A THUNDER CITY NOVELLA

A SECRET
LIFE

DEBRA JESS

1

During the grand finale of Blood Hunter

"GET DOWN. YOU KNOW BETTER." Evan Blackwood took his hand off the electric can opener to remove the offending feline from the kitchen counter. He could have used his Alt ability to lift the cat off, but animals in general didn't react well to him manipulating air molecules.

The three beasts acted as if they hadn't been fed in days. In reality, the menagerie had eaten before dawn because he couldn't sleep and needed the distraction. The cats hadn't cared about the extra early hour and had scarfed down last night's leftover hamburger.

When he had finally fallen asleep, his nightmares returned, tossing and turning him until he'd woken up again a few minutes ago.

The cats hadn't cared about his nightmares, either. They demanded a second breakfast by pouncing on his chest at their usual time. The tortoiseshell, Crete, even had the audacity to dig a claw into Evan's nose, forcing him out from under the sweat-soaked sheets.

He hadn't been home for most of the past two weeks—abandoning them, as far as they were concerned.

Evan filled three individual bowls with the premium wet stuff and placed them on the floor, two of them together at one side of the kitchen island and the third at the opposite end. If he placed all three together, the two older bullies would eat the food of the youngest. Then he cleaned the counter before pulling out fish food for his aquariums from the cabinets above, followed by pellets for his gerbils.

Keeping the gerbils in an apartment filled with cats was a challenge. The animal rescue group he worked with had found a dozen of them in a home raided by the police. There weren't many takers for gerbils, but the rescue group swore up, down, and sideways they would find the critters a forever home.

In the background, the television droned. The white noise kept him focused on his chores, and off himself. He didn't want to think about himself or remember...

As the memory loop started again, he dropped the bag of gerbil pellets and jammed the palms of his hands into his eyes.

The explosion had broken his concentration before the shock wave hit him from behind. The cargo container he and his twin brother, Alek, were balancing in mid-air started to slip. Alek's face switched from casual focus to absolute horror. If the container fell, it would crush everyone below them. No sooner had Evan registered what had gone wrong than metal debris slammed into him. His Alt ability wavered even more, unable to keep hold of the container.

White light behind his eyes obscured his vision, the pain more intense than anything he'd ever experienced. Alek screamed his name, helpless to stop Evan from falling, his bones breaking when he hit the deck. Flames licked his uniform, then his skin. By instinct alone, he ignored his broken bones and shoved away the air molecules surrounding him.

Starving the fire of oxygen meant he had almost no air to breathe. With his eyes closed against the heat, he couldn't tell how far back he'd pushed the flames. He could only lie there, gulping with his failing strength what few super-heated molecules had slipped past his barrier, hoping his teammates would save him before he lost consciousness.

The power he exerted to keep himself alive made him blind to everything else. At some point his mother, still wet from keeping the cargo ship afloat, pulled him above the firestorm before flying him home instead of to the hospital.

She was going to ask Hannah Quinn to heal him, but the charred skin on his face made it impossible for him to talk her out of it. Captain Spectacular had almost lost two sons—Nik and Cory—in the past two weeks. He couldn't blame her for ignoring protocol, and her own directive, by asking Hannah to do the one thing the Blood Surfer wasn't supposed to do.

Whether the Oversight Committee and the people of Thunder City agreed with his mother's decision was a problem for another day.

A loud chime jolted him out of the nightmare. With sweat-soaked hands, he pulled his comm from its clip on his jeans. Messages for Thunder City's Alt Support Services, T-CASS, poured across the screen in rapid succession as the teams assembled.

A bomb threat had been called in. The target: Harbor Regional Hospital. The operations manager demanded silence during the evacuation. No sirens, no flashing lights. A final message sank his heart: his stepfather, Thomas Carraro, had been shot.

Evan scrolled faster. No orders for him, though, and no orders for Alek. Both he and his brother were grounded since everyone believed they were still recovering from the harbor attack. Evan checked his phone for personal messages. Nothing yet. His mother would be in the thick of the evacuation, and his eldest brother, Nik, knew how to deactivate bombs. He wouldn't hear from them until the threat was over.

Along with his family, the usual team members responded: Blockhead, Mach Ten, Seeker, Flame, Spritz. Evan couldn't help but notice that Gillian hadn't responded. Headquarters more than likely hadn't summoned her. Their loss. Like Spritz, Gillian could control water molecules. Unlike Spritz, Gillian had been born with gills so she could breathe under water. That's why the public had chosen the moniker "Gilly" when she officially joined T-CASS. She spent most of her time in Mystic Bay or working at the city's aquarium. Despite assisting in saving his life during the harbor attack, no one had thought to summon her to a land-based terrorist attack at the hospital.

Evan's thumb hovered over the comm. Should he remind HQ that Gillian was an important member of the team? That she also had superhuman strength? Would Gillian appreciate him bringing her to the attention of the operations team?

Probably not. Gillian didn't appear to like people too much and he hadn't seen her at HQ in almost a month.

Actually, until now, he hadn't realized that he'd been looking for her at HQ when he was there.

Evan clamped down on the extra thump from his heart. Now wasn't the time for thinking about a woman, especially a teammate. Not that it mattered, since Gillian had only dated women since joining T-CASS, a fact he only knew because he'd asked around about her. No one at T-CASS seemed to know her well enough for further details, so he'd left the possibility of dating her alone.

In the living room, the news reporter on the screen was live downtown. Evan grabbed the fish food and gerbil pellets while he listened to the broadcast.

"Yes, that's all we know at this point. Terrorists have placed bombs all around Harbor Regional Hospital. T-CASS and the police have responded. They are evacuating the hospital as quickly as possible, and all traffic is detoured. If you need emergency care, here are the alternatives..."

Feeding the fish tugged him away from the temptation to respond to the messages despite not receiving orders. Still, the instinct to do something, anything, remained. His comm pinged before that thought went any further, and a priority icon popped up. A private message from his mother for him and Alek.

Don't you two even think about it. Stay away. I'll contact you if I need you.

Evan dropped the comm onto the sofa and headed toward his bedroom, where he had two more fish tanks, his annoyance at war with the logic of his mother's message. He could only assume that his mother didn't want to advertise the fact that Hannah had broken the law on behalf of the Blackwoods.

There was nothing he could do about it. He didn't dare interrupt his mother during an operation to complain. She would share any information about Thomas when she had time.

If Thomas died....

Worrying about something before it happened served no purpose, so Evan moved on to the spare bedroom where he had set up the gerbil cages. He knew how much his mother would be hurt if Thomas died, and he would support her no matter what. Unlike Alek, Evan had made peace with Thomas a long time ago.

Finished feeding his pets, Evan returned to the living room and scooped up Kea, the calico, so he could sit on the sofa while he called his brother. Mykonos, the Russian Blue curled up next to him. Alek didn't answer on his first attempt, so Evan called again, and kept calling until Alek finally answered.

"You're not responding to your comm," Evan said.

The background noise ceased, so Alek must have silenced one of his video games. "I just woke up. We're on medical leave until Mom says otherwise. No one should be contacting us via the comm."

"There's been an attack on Harbor Regional Hospital." Evan paused. "Thomas has been shot. Mom is down there with Nik. Someone's planted bombs around the hospital."

Evan waited, hoping Alek wouldn't brush off the shooting because it was Thomas and not one of their teammates.

"I'll be ready in five," Alek said. "You can meet me at the corner of—"

"No way." Evan interrupted his brother's plan, though he was relieved that Alek was ready for action. "We can't go down there. Mom's orders. Check your damn comm."

He waited again while Alek found their mother's message. "All right. We won't go downtown, but we can still go to HQ."

"If you want." Evan knew exactly why Alek wanted to go to HQ. Serena would be working with the Star Haven Newcomers. She was the one person Alek cared about more than their family. He'd have to needle his brother about it another day. "But use the roof entrance and don't wear your uniform. I think Mom's more worried about advertising our rapid recovery than she is about our health."

"Will you meet me there?" Alek asked.

So, he could watch Alek make a fool of himself pursuing Nik's longtime and very ex-fiancée? No way was he going to put himself in the middle of that drama, not even for his twin. "No. I'm going to the clinic. They're shorthanded as it is. I'm heading there now. Text me if you learn anything new at HQ."

"Will do." Alek hung up.

Evan clipped his comm and phone to his jeans. He gave Kea a quick scratch behind her ears before heading out to the deck. His apartment overlooked West Ashland Park and was a quick five-minute flight to the veterinary practice where he worked part-time.

Adding power to the wind, Evan created a vortex to launch himself toward the sky. He climbed over the top of the apartment building, then banked toward the Bayside neighborhood.

He'd only been flying for a few minutes when a shock wave hit, followed by a muffled boom. The wave wasn't powerful enough to knock him off course, but he stopped mid-flight to figure out where it had originated. In the distance, the clouds rippled as smoke billowed out over downtown.

Alek! The university district was closer to Harbor Regional than he was. If Alek had launched at the same time he had...

The scent of sugar cookies filled his nose.

Alek is fine, Evan.

Pathia.

The shock wave only knocked him off course. His first concern was for the Captain, then you.

Evan flashed images of the rest of his family through his mind, a quick way to ask Pathia about their status.

They are all fine, except I cannot find Hannah. I'm not able to read her, but that may not mean anything—I'm not as familiar with her thoughts as I am with yours and your family's. An ambulance is transporting Thomas to the Fargrounds Medical Center. I'll keep looking for Hannah, I promise.

Thunder City would riot if Hannah died.

Keep going, Evan. I've got this. If something happens, I'll let you know.

Evan visualized a bouquet of flowers for Pathia. The scent of sugar cookies grew stronger for a second, then disappeared. Evan looked back at the downtown skyline.

The memory loop started again.

Pain.

Flames.

No oxygen.

Dying.

Without focus, he lost control of his vortex and tumbled head over heel, barely catching himself before he hit the ground. He had to get out of here and find someplace to escape his thoughts.

From this height, he could just about see the edge of Silvergrass Pier. This time of day there would be a handful of fishermen, but if he settled himself on the boulders shoring up the wooden structure, no one would bother him. It took a supreme amount of focus to get his mind off his family and fly toward the shore. Mystic Bay reflected the early morning sun along calm waters. As he suspected, there was only one fisherman, and he appeared to be packing up his equipment in a hurry. Maybe he'd heard the explosion? Did he know someone who worked downtown? Evan's fear turned to anger. No one should have to have their lives disrupted at the whims of the hate-mongers.

Still, he now had the entire pier to himself, so he flew to the point. Instead of lowering himself onto one of the boulders, he hovered in place, his back to both the harbor and the heart of Thunder City.

Over the horizon sat Star Haven, but he ignored that nasty source of Thunder City's troubles, and just watched the calm waves roll toward the shore. In the distance, a few dolphins leapt out of the water, diving back in without a care in the world. Maybe this was why Gillian spent more time swimming in the bay rather than interacting with her teammates. Under the water's surface, what could go wrong? It would be cold but peaceful, with no anti-Alts trying to kill him or his family.

He let his imagination wander, finding a little inner peace, until something slammed into his head.

Pain.

Flames.

No oxygen.

Dying.

He fell toward the boulders below.

GILLIAN SANDS SKIMMED along the port side of the half-sunken cargo ship, the water shifting with the tide and her mood. The initial assumption reported by the crime scene investigators didn't hold up from she saw. Their description said that only one container carried explosives and that was enough to tear apart the main deck and engine room. From under the surface, it appeared as if there had been several bombs planted in different locations. Whoever activated them had done so with the intent of creating maximum damage, not caring who died, Alts or Norms. Once the Captain had stopped lifting the ship from underneath, it sank further into Mystic Bay.

Gillian never thanked T-CASS for overlooking her during emergency operations, and today was no different. When the dispatcher had given her the assignment, she jumped at the opportunity, eager to represent T-CASS in an actual investigation and have a personal hand in striking a blow against Star Haven.

Then the dispatcher told her T-CASS only wanted her to take pictures. There wasn't even a deadline to write up a report. Her thoughts and opinions meant nothing. Just turn in the camera and let the professionals take care of the rest.

The harbor police dive team should be handling this, but it was faster for her to do it. She didn't need oxygen tanks because of her gills. Her superior strength let her access parts of the ship blocked by mangled metal, and no detail, even in the murkiest conditions, escaped her eyesight. Oh, sure, they might notice her when she teamed up with Spritz to create water jets to put out a fire, but it was Spritz they called when a land-based operation went down, not "Gilly" who was only needed for threats in Mystic Bay. Thunder City needed her because of her body, not her brains.

Not that Star Haven was much better. As far as she was concerned, Star Haven was the architect of all of this misery, and they could drown in it for all she cared. Her parents had fled Star Haven and settled in Thunder City when their neighbors discovered they had a four-year-old with gills.

It irked her that once again, Thunder City didn't think she could do anything other than patrol Mystic Bay.

In fact, no one ever asked her to do anything that didn't involve swimming. If she did accept the rare invitation to go out, whoever she was with would spend all evening trying not to stare at her neck instead of looking at *her*.

The only exception was Evan Blackwood.

Every time he looked at her, his elevator eyes traveled from her chest to her hips then to her legs, his sexy smile growing wider every second. It was stupid. The one man in Thunder City who ignored her gills was the one man who had also bedded almost every woman along the shore and beyond, according to *The Sizzler*. With her, he looked but never touched.

Why he kept his distance despite his obvious interest was a mystery. It wasn't as if she would turn down a tumble with Rumble. Who wouldn't want to curl into his strong arms and feel his sculpted body pressed against them? She hadn't had a relationship with a man since high school, when her prom date ditched her at the last minute for a cheerleader—a Norm cheerleader. After that, sticking to women wasn't a hardship, but changing dating tactics hadn't increased her chances for a long-term relationship.

The fact that Evan was interested and didn't do anything about it was an insult, wasn't it?

Maybe he'd never asked her out because she was a colleague, though she was pretty sure he'd slept with other T-CASS members. Was it because she was too young? He was twenty-six, three years older, which wasn't *that* much of a difference. Was it because she came from a solid middle-class neighborhood and his family lived in a house larger than a cruise ship?

More than likely, he simply wasn't any different from everyone else. Not that it mattered. Evan had fallen into the inferno on the ship. She hadn't heard what had happened to him after Captain Spec lifted him to safety, but Gillian couldn't imagine he'd escaped without breaking more than a few bones.

If he had asked her out before the attack, no one would question why she wanted to know about his recovery. But he hadn't, so all she knew was what the news reported, which was next to nothing.

Her anger at past slights slipped away under the weight of her concern for Evan. The best thing she could do right now was follow orders.

Point and shoot, point and shoot, she took picture after picture of the scorched hull. What little speculation she'd heard was that the anti-Alts were looking to destroy the evidence of Mayor Dane's quarry prison, and the high body count was just an added bonus.

So much terror in such a short span of time. She and Spritz had teamed up during the attack, both of them creating steady streams of water from the bay and aiming them toward the blaze. It wasn't easy, because they also had to avoid drowning the crew, not to mention Evan.

If I accidentally drowned Evan...

No, the sick feeling in her in her stomach steered her away from that thought.

A school of trout swam past her arm, tickling her skin with their fins, interrupting her dark thoughts. Since no one wanted a report on her findings, there was nothing for her to do after she turned over the camera. Maybe she'd return to the Mystic Bay to find the dolphin pod she had played with yesterday. Dolphins knew how to have fun, and they didn't care about what she looked like. One of the juveniles had won the game by snagging a colorful scarf she'd brought with her for a game of tag.

With the exterior examination of the ship finished, Gillian climbed onto what was left of the main deck. This particular cargo ship only had three holds, and all of them flooded. One hold had held the refrigerated remains of the gigantic mutant Alt Miranda Dane had created. The anti-Alts never considered that the Blackwood twins would work alongside the Norm longshoremen on something as mundane as removing cargo containers.

Rule number one in Thunder City: never underestimated the determination of Rumble and Roar to get the job done. Both sacrificed their bodies to get the container onto the boardwalk without letting it fall on top of anyone. They had saved so many lives through their sheer force of will and determination. Even someone as jaded as she was could admire their strength, though deep down, her heart ached for Evan. He must have suffered severe burns, on top of broken bones, when he fell into the inferno. It would be a long time before she would have the opportunity to see him again.

Since the container with the body had been removed from the first cargo hold, Gillian dove right in, grateful she didn't have to worry about swimming through body parts. She took pictures of the damage and jumped right back out again. The second hold had contained only the weapons used by Miranda Dane's mercenaries. Gillian jumped in again with her camera and finished even faster than she had with the first hold.

Back on deck, she took a moment to stretch. The rising summer sun made days like this feel hot and lazy. Gillian glanced at the third hold, tempted to skip it since it was empty and had been farthest from the blast. Instead, she resisted temptation and used her superhuman strength one more time to open the hatch.

This hold had such a foul stench to it, Gillian almost changed her mind. Still, the first two hadn't taken long, so this one shouldn't be any different. Closing her throat and opening her gills, Gillian lowered herself into the water.

Almost immediately, something brushed her arm. She looked back, expecting to see another school of trout or striped bass. Instead, she saw a human face, its dead eyes staring back at her.

Bile burned her throat. She'd never had contact with a dead human body before, and every preliminary report she'd read said the entire ship's crew and all the passengers had survived the blast. She tried to circle around the body without touching its free-floating arms, her camera recording everything. She had almost made it to the feet when the second body appeared in her peripheral vision. A third bumped into the second a little farther beyond, then a fourth, then a fifth. A sixth body, smaller than the others, floated underneath the others with a teddy bear peeking out from a coat pocket.

Gillian plowed downward, finding more bodies and snapping pictures until she was sure she'd documented them all. Then she shot upwards, past the floating horror show, leaping out of the hold in a wild trajectory and landing hard on the deck. Her body, frozen in shock, refused to move. Puking with her throat closed would suffocate her. It took a full minute of kneeling with her gills flaring until she could force her throat open and breathe. Breathing calmed her down, but she kept her head bowed and her eyes closed while her stomach churned.

Another minute passed. Convinced her stomach had settled, Gillian stood, so she could hook the camera to the belt of her moss-green uniform before running toward the port side of the ship and diving back into the bay.

The open water cleansed her as she swam faster and faster, trying to purge the images in her mind. The last thing she expected to see was a familiar silhouette hovering over Silvergrass Pier, watching the horizon. How could it be either one of the twins since they had both been wounded during the attack?

She'd have to ask about that later. From this angle, she saw only the man's profile, but she immediately knew it was Evan. Side by side, the brothers were almost indistinguishable unless you knew what to look for. Evan's smile resembled a beluga while Alek's looked more like that of a shark. Evan also held himself with casual ease, inviting people to approach, while Alek kept his arms crossed, challenging the world to mess with him.

With Evan here, she could use his comm to call in the emergency crew, instead of waiting until she could dig her own comm out of her gym bag, which was locked in her truck on the far side of the parking lot.

"Evan!"

Nothing, not even a twitch. Mystic Bay had its share of seagulls, crashing waves, and wind, and her voice was always compromised for a minute or two after she'd been submerged. She tried again.

"Evan!"

Still nothing. She had to get closer, so she dove deep enough to generate power to hurl herself onto the pier. Perfect landing, almost directly under Evan. Once she straightened up, she closed her gills, opened her throat, took the biggest breath she could.

"Ev-an Black-wood!"

Over-enunciating didn't work either. What on earth had caught his attention that kept him from hearing her? Directing her control over the water molecules, she launched a spout and aimed it directly at the back of Evan's head.

_____

DON'T LET ME BURN!

Evan's fear froze his control over the vortex, his brain reacting to the shock of the attack before his body could adjust. He had no time to create a new vortex and shift it under his body. Tumbling, Evan knew he was going to hit the pier, breaking every bone in his body—again.

"Oooph. Fucking hell, stop floundering."

Who said that? And why wasn't he in screaming pain? Evan tried to sit up, but he wasn't flat on his back as he had expected. A pair of pretty gold eyes surrounded by spiky hair stared down at him. Strong arms pulled him close against a damp body.

"What the hell, Gillian?" Evan shifted in her arms, but she held him tight. "You damn near killed me."

"I'm sorry. I'm so, so sorry. I had to get your attention and you were just staring into the distance. You didn't hear me shouting your name. I swear, I didn't mean to hit you that hard."

She lowered him to the pier so he could scramble onto his feet. His soaked clothes now clung to his body. He ignored his discomfort because he could tell something was really wrong with Gillian. She wrapped her arms around herself, shaking, which seemed unusual for someone who could wrestle him to the ground without breaking a sweat. He wouldn't have minded her tackling him now, except she wouldn't be interested in him like that.

"Dead bodies in the wreck." She stopped talking to take a deep breath. "At least twenty-five, one of them a child."

Evan stopped wondering how soft Gillian's gills would feel under his touch. "How is that possible? The crew and the Star Haven delegates were accounted for. It's a cargo ship, not a passenger ship."

Gillian took one more breath. "I don't know. I just know what I saw. I took pictures. Please, let me use your comm."

Evan snatched the comm off his belt, hoping it still worked after the dousing. Gillian grabbed it from him, but the device slipped in her wet hands. She swore, then closed her eyes. He could see what she was doing. He manipulated air molecules, but she controlled water, so she was using her ability to pull the water off her hands and wetsuit. His jeans stopped clinging to his thighs, and he could no longer feel cold droplets down the back of his shirt.

He listened to her report without comment. He still couldn't believe T-CASS had missed so many people. Why were they in the hold in the first place? Why were there *children* down there?

Gillian handed him back the comm. "Thanks. I need to get back over there."

She turned to dive into the bay.

"Whoa." He reached out to grab her arm. "Wait a second."

"What?" She faced him again, surprised that he'd stopped her.

"You can't go back."

"Watch me."

She bent her knees preparing to leap into the water again, but this time Evan lifted off, so he could block her from the other side of the guard rails. "Gillian, listen to me. There's a procedure for this."

"I can't leave those poor people down there. They deserve better."

"And they'll get it. T-CASS will report your findings to the harbor police. They have their own divers who can retrieve the bodies and bring them to where they can be properly handled."

"But..."

"What are you going to do? Haul them onto the boardwalk and leave them there to rot until emergency services picks them up? The ship is a crime scene. Let the police do their jobs."

She opened her mouth, then closed it again. "The harbor police are Norms."

Uh-oh. Gillian's tone of voice stopped Evan cold. In a city built on cultivating trust between normal and alternative humans, there wasn't a lot of wiggle room for hate, especially by a member of T-CASS. Any hatred had serious consequences in Thunder City.

"Do you really want to have this argument with me?"

Her mouth softened. "You're right. I'm sorry. I wasn't thinking. I'm just so damn mad right now."

Maybe she was telling the truth, or maybe she knew better than to spew hatred toward Norms at Catherine Blackwood's son. Evan had said similar things once, thanks to a grandfather who had tried to warp him and his brothers into believing they were superior. His mother had taken care of that problem over a decade ago. No one had seen his grandfather since.

If Gillian truly had an anti-Norm attitude, then she had a bigger problem than twenty-five dead bodies. The dead could be handled within the hour. Prejudice took a lot longer to heal, and sometimes trying to fix it didn't work.

Either way, Evan would keep an eye on her, which was no hardship if she really were just tired. "I don't blame you, but your work is done. If you want to help the divers, I'm sure they won't refuse, but right now Thunder City has bigger problems."

"Bigger problems than twenty-five dead people?"

She didn't know about the hospital. How could she if she'd been in the water all afternoon? "There's been another attempted bombing at Harbor Regional."

This time her fists clenched with rage she didn't even try to hide. "Damned Norms."

"It's the anti-Alts," he said, trying to make her see the difference.

"Same thing."

"It's not the same thing." The urge to offer an outlet for her anger prodded him to take a step closer. "C'mon, Gillian, let's get off the pier. We can meet the harbor police at the warehouse, and you can explain your findings in detail to them."

The look on her face could have split the boulders shoring up the pier. Without another word, she turned away from him and stomped toward the parking lot.

He walked beside her rather than fly, though her long stride down the wooden boards was so fast, he had to double time his own to catch up to her. "If it were the same thing, we wouldn't have Rocklin Prison full of Alt prisoners. Alts commit crimes too."

"We're not trying to murder every Norm in existence."

"How do you know those people you just found aren't Norms?" he asked. "A moment ago, you said they deserved better."

"They're not Norms." Gillian shook her head, not looking at him. Her determination centered on getting to her vehicle. "They can't be. Why would Norms be in the hold of a cargo ship? If they were part of the Star Haven delegation, they would have disembarked along with the acting mayor. If they were part of the crew, they would have been on deck unloading the containers. There is...was a child down there. They had to have been hiding, and if they were hiding, why would Norms have to hide themselves on board a cargo ship to escape a city that passed an Alt-ban?"

She had him there. It made sense that the Alts still trapped in Star Haven would smuggle themselves out of the city to avoid arrest, especially now that the details of Miranda Dane's illegal prison were known. Just because Dane was dead didn't mean that her legacy in Star Haven wouldn't live on.

Evan ran a few lengths to catch up with Gillian again. "Okay, so they were Alts trying to escape the Alt ban because they couldn't get out of the city in time. Why this ship? It was crewed by Norms."

"We don't know that for sure though, do we?"

They'd reached the stairs leading down to the near-empty parking lot. Chipped paint scratched the palms of his hands as he slid them down the railing. Gillian was still in the lead, her destructive thought process keeping him by her side.

If his mother, Catherine Blackwood—Captain Spectacular —was unaware of Gillian's opinion of Norms, then there was a still a chance he could change her mind before his mother found out. If his mother could drive her own father out of the city—banish him, in fact—because of his attitude toward Norms and what he was teaching her sons, who the hell knew what she would do with a T-CASS member? Gillian would lose her job at the very least.

Evan didn't want to see that happen; though, at the moment he couldn't say exactly why he felt so strongly about keeping Gillian on the team. Keeping her near him.

Hello. You don't have what she wants, so cool it. It's not like you're going to be bedding a woman anytime soon. Not with Thomas shot and Thunder City in chaos. If Thomas dies, Mom is going to want all of us back home.

He hoped Thomas wouldn't die. Yeah, his own father was alive, and he was grateful for that, but his mother had lost her second husband and for months after, she could barely function outside of work, both for T-CASS and for Blackwood Enterprises. He didn't want her going through that sort of pain again. She didn't deserve it. No one did.

They made it to Gillian's truck, a pickup with the Thunder City seaquarium logo on the side. "I'm going to the warehouse to meet the divers," she said. "If you want to join me, you're welcome to. Either way, I'm gone."

"You can't drive over there. The parking lot is part of the crime scene. I'll fly you over." The look of embarrassment over having forgotten why she'd parked at the pier in the first place tinged her pale cheeks for a second, before it was replaced by the look everyone got about how cool it would be to fly. Except he could tell Gillian didn't want to enjoy it under the circumstances. "It'll be fine. I've never dropped anyone."

Except yourself, into the flames while Alek watched.

The damned loop started again. His body twitched as the flames reached out for him and he couldn't bring in the air he needed to keep himself aloft under control.

"You okay?"

Gillian's voice was drowned under the noise of a crackling wildfire. Flames were everywhere, reaching for him, the skin on his back burning. He could smell his own flesh cooking.

Though the flames, he could see an escape. A tunnel with gold at the end. Soft eyes that could see into his soul, offering comfort.

He reached to find a way out, but his hand found Gillian's cheek instead—smooth, cool skin where heat should have been, but wasn't. The loop ended and Evan realized what he'd done, and how foolish he must look, touching her as if she was more than just a colleague who needed him. He couldn't let her know that, though. She might take it the wrong way, so he jerked his hand away.

"Yeah, I'm fine. We should leave now if we're going to meet the dive team."

He could still see the look of concern on her face. It confirmed what he thought: Gillian was a good person, but something must have happened to sour her attitude toward Norms. Finding out what it was before she said the wrong thing to the wrong person would give him an excuse to get to know her better. Just as friends, of course, because that's all she would want.

He, after all, had a reputation to uphold as the friendlier half of Rumble and Roar, and Gillian stood closer than necessary for him to carry her.

"Ready?" he asked.

She nodded. "All right. Let's do this."

He generated a vortex, starting at their feet and working up their waists. "Lean into it."

She did and with a swoosh, he lifted her into the air.

GILLIAN DIDN'T LIKE the look that came over Evan's face when he had touched her cheek. He was remembering something painful, that was obvious, and she had a good guess as to what it was. The pained expression had tightened his features, sharpened them, made her want to rescue him from whatever it was. She hadn't known at first that he had been the twin who'd fallen into the fire. She'd found out later, after reading the preliminary reports, and figured that the new Alt in town, the one they called the Blood Surfer, had healed him. But even that couldn't have made the memories of almost burning alive any easier.

Of course, she was only guessing. There were a lot of reasons for Evan not to want to touch her. Maybe her gills had flared, and he'd noticed, because the second he touched her skin, a shot of desire shivered down her spine.

Whatever. If her gills hadn't flared before, they sure as hell flared now. She was flying!

The sensation of cool air passing over her skin didn't detract from the view of the water from overhead. She couldn't help the instinct to close her throat, so she couldn't breathe through her nose or mouth, like she did whenever she dove into Mystic Bay. After a minute though, her head swum, and her vision darkened. *Idiot. You can breathe just fine up here with your lungs.* She relaxed her muscles and drew in air like she normally would on land. The dizzy sensation cleared away, leaving her with nothing but a magnificent view of water and of Evan.

Whatever bothered Evan before had left. How could anything trouble you so far above everything? Sometimes, when she was depressed or upset, she'd dive straight to the bottom of the bay and look up at the refraction of sunlight filtering through the water. The kaleidoscope would mesmerize her until all the bad feelings retreated far enough for her to think without hurt.

Evan hadn't appeared to judge her either, though she didn't know him well enough to guess why. She only went to headquarters when she had to. Even with all of the events of the past two weeks, she hadn't been called on for any of the raids except the harbor attack. Just as well. She could read the operations reports from the comfort of her own apartment while still in her pajamas. That was the best way to get through those reports. No one could see her get angry and call her out for hating Norms. No one could accuse her of not doing her job because of how she felt.

Almost as soon as the flight started, it came to an end.

Silvergrass Pier wasn't that far from the harbor. And while the harbor was long, Evan took the route over the bay, so it made the flight shorter. Evan landed them on the dock, not far from where the divers had mustered. Some were already donning their gear. She wanted to thank Evan, not just for staying with her, but for giving her enough separation from the horror inside the ship that she might be able to talk to the harbor police without biting her tongue. Before she could though, his comm chimed.

One of the divers approached them while Evan checked his message.

"Gilly?" the diver asked.

"Yes, that's me." *No, it isn't.* She smiled through gritted teeth just the same.

"Your verbal report said twenty-five bodies are in one of the holds?"

"Correct. I can lead you to them."

"We'd be appreciative if you did." He nodded toward his team. "It will make retrieving them a lot faster. We'll be ready to board in five." He moved toward the edge of the dock to wait on her.

Using the word *appreciative* eased her annoyance somewhat, but she wouldn't dive until she made sure Evan would be okay. He clipped his comm back onto his jeans.

"That was Mom. Thomas is out of surgery. He'll be okay."

He looked relieved, so Gillian gave him a gentle nudge with her elbow. "I'm glad to hear it."

"Are you? Thomas is a Norm, remember."

Oh, dear. Evan might play the big, dumb oversexed playboy, but he was a lot sharper than he let on. Most of the time, she knew better than to spew what she really felt about Norms in front of her T-CASS colleagues, but doing so in front of a Blackwood? In front of Evan? Not one of her better moments.

"Yes, I remember." She left it at that. Anything more and she risked digging herself in deeper. For some reason she didn't want Evan to see her as anti-Norm. Even though she was, wasn't she?

The dive commander motioned toward her, so she joined them as they boarded the ship, Evan following though he didn't have to. As soon as she opened the hold again, the team flipped off the deck, diving deep.

"I need to get in the water."

If Evan expected more from her about Thomas, he didn't indicate it. "I'll wait here."

"You don't have to do that."

He shrugged. "Maybe I want to. I can help bring the bodies back onto the dock."

"Okay. I'll find you as soon as we're finished."

The dive took a long time. The bloated bodies floated like ghosts. Some had lost limbs in the blast; others still had their eyes open. The gruesome scene made her retch again. She fought it, damned if she would let Norms see her weakness, and tried to focus on the clothes of the dead, so she wouldn't have to see the faces.

She used her control over the water to help bring the bodies to the surface, where the other officers pulled them out and lined them up side by side. By the time she had finished, another squad of harbor police had covered the bodies with tarps. Rather than ask for an assist getting out of the hold, she dove down and used her powerful legs to leap out of the water, close to where Evan waited.

He backed away to avoid the water spray.

"You got all of them?"

"Yeah. The harbor police should still check the general area, just to make sure...there are no more. I can't...twenty-five people dead. Their faces...I could see their eyes. They were trapped...rising water...no way to escape...." She choked trying to talk with her throat not quite clear yet. Once her throat opened and she gulped air, she tried to talk, but couldn't quite find the words she needed. Evan noticed her struggle and opened his arms.

"C'mere."

She took his offered invitation, and stepped into his hug, realizing too late that he'd get wet all over again. Well, maybe this way he wouldn't notice her tears soaking his t-shirt. He just held her, not saying anything, just rocking her back and forth.

"Kids," she sobbed. "There were kids down there."

"I'm so sorry you had to see that, Gillian."

She pulled out of his arms, her breathing a little steadier, but she had to wipe her eyes anyway. "Thanks for this."

"Anytime." He sounded as if he meant it too. She hoped he did, because being held by Evan felt...nice.

The officer who had approached them earlier, walked over to her again. "Thanks for all of your help, Gilly. Without you, it would have taken us twice as long. We're going to get the bodies downtown for processing. We'll see if we can identify them."

"They're Alts." Gillian was more convinced of that then before. "My guess is they couldn't get out before the Alt ban and were trying to escape from Star Haven."

He nodded. "We'll get an investigation started, though it might take a while with everything that's happened today. There's still a list of missing Alts the Newcomers constructed for us. We'll see if Star Haven will share info with us if needed."

He held out a hand to shake hers. Hesitating in front in front of Evan, after her earlier gaff, wasn't an option, but she couldn't help it. She tried to cover her mistake by holding her hands up, making a show of drying them, then shaking the Norm's hand. Had Evan noticed? She hoped not, but had to wait for the officer to walk away before turning back to Evan. His face didn't give away what he was thinking.

"I should get back to the truck and return it to the seaquarium," she said, in hopes of running away from the awkward situation.

"How do you feel about cats?"

What an odd question. "Uh, I like them well enough, I guess. I've never owned one."

Evan jerked his chin toward the pier in the distance. "Why don't we return the truck, then we could go back to my place. I have three cats, three aquariums, and six gerbils."

"Gerbils?"

"Rescues. I'm keeping them until we can find them a home."

She thought about the offer, but the dead floated into her mind's eye. Going home to an empty apartment lost all appeal, and swimming alone in the bay, which usually calmed her down, couldn't drain the sadness from her heart. "I guess so."

"I mean, the fish and gerbils won't bother you, but the cats are demanding little beasts. You'll have to hug them, and pet them, and squeeze them..."

That made her laugh. "Are you sure they're cats and not bunny rabbits?"

He flashed the smile that had melted hearts all over the city, sometimes two or three per night according the news rags. Still, it would be better than going back to her own apartment and stewing about the bodies, remembering their faces. Would she even be able to get to sleep again? "Okay, cat whispering it is."

He stepped close to her, closer than he had when they were on the pier. "Ready?"

She could fly again. Even if this was a mistake, she could at least get one more flight and forget her nightmares.

"I'm ready. Let's go."

Her feet left the ground, but her heart soared.

3

EVAN LANDED on the deck outside the apartment with Gillian right next to him. He was glad she'd agreed to join him. Her face had held twenty-five nightmares he wanted to banish. He suspected his own nightmare gave him the same look. Why did he keep remembering the fire? Maybe that's why he had extended his offer, so that they could forget together. Or, if not forget, at least face the dread, stomp it into the ground, then move on?

He hoped so. He didn't want to spend the rest of his life zoning out. What if it happened during an operation? Someone could die because he wasn't paying attention.

When he was a teenager, he'd almost killed his youngest brother, Cory. After the incident, he had still never truly understood why Cory had left the family, why he ran away to an anti-Alt city like Star Haven.

Now, he knew exactly why his brother had left. Even though Evan had apologized, and he and Cory were working together on their relationship, it wasn't the same as when they were kids.

Nothing would ever be the same. Not after all they had been through.

"Look at them." Gillian dropped her gym bag and knelt in front of the sliding glass doors. The cats somehow always knew when he landed out here. They were pawing at the door, demanding that he open it and let them out. He sometimes did, but only when he had the time to keep an eye on them. The deck wrapped around the building and the cats loved to sit on the handrail and sun themselves. The last thing he needed was for one of them to roll off and fall twelve stories if he wasn't there to catch them with a vortex.

He slid the door open to let the cats scamper. Instead of heading for the handrails, they started sniffing at Gillian's ankles.

"You smell fish, don't you?" Her laugh jingled like a pretty tune while she knelt to run her hands down Crete's sleek back. "You think I'm going to give you a can of tuna."

"You sure know how to charm a land animal. Tuna is mana from the gods."

Kea took the advantage of her bent knees, climbing higher to lick at her gills. She pulled the cat away. "Not the gills, darling, those are sensitive."

Sensitive, huh. He filed that information away. He told himself it was good to know if your colleague had a weakness, just in case it affected an operation. It wasn't like he was going to sleep with her, or anything. He had to wonder though, just how her gills would react if he ran his thumb along their soft edges?

He picked up the offender in his own arms, but the scamp started to squirm. "Why don't you go inside and get changed out of your uniform. If you head down the hallway, there's a spare bedroom across from mine and next to my office. Use the shower if you like."

She squinted in the sun; her head tilted to the side as if thinking about what he was asking her to do. He had no ulterior motive other than the fact that wearing a wet suit for so many hours had to be uncomfortable if you weren't in the water swimming. The look on her face didn't appear irritated, though.

"Or we can stay out here if you like," he said, hoping that she would agree. "I can bring you something to drink. There are snacks too if you're hungry."

"No, I'm sorry, I got distracted." She bent down to disengage herself from Kea's claws, before picking up the gym bag and slinging it over her shoulder. "I must be more tired than I thought. I could use a shower and a change of clothes. And a snack sounds lovely. Something fattening and sweet. I think we both deserve it after the day we've had."

He waited until she was inside and down the hallway before wrangling the cats back where they belonged. In the kitchen, he checked the pantry and found popcorn, which he popped in the microwave. There were chips and salsa in the cupboard, enough to fill two bowls. Crete, as usual, jumped on the counter to check out the offerings.

What else? Would she prefer soda? Or, something more relaxing, like wine? He had a bottle of dry white, but she'd asked for fattening and sweet. He dug into his pantry for a box of dark chocolate and put a pan on the stove. Within moments, he had melted the chocolate, added cream and some sweetener, and then pulled out a bottle of vodka. A little decadent, but it was his favorite drink when he was feeling blue. Maybe it would soothe Gillian the way it did him? He hoped so.

He served the whole affair on the dining room table, just as Gillian reappeared. God, she looked tempting in her tight-fitting black yoga pants and crop top. Her hair was combed back, thick with a curl around her ears. But it was her eyes that mesmerized him. He'd seen them before, but never up close and very personal.

What was he thinking? She'd slug him if she knew where his thoughts were wandering. Instead of continuing to torture himself by looking at her, he fussed with setting out napkins and pouring the hot chocolate. One of the cats jumped onto a seat. That was fine, as long as they kept their mitts off the tabletop.

"What's all this?" She licked her lips.

He'd guessed right. She was hungry but had lost her appetite recovering the bodies.

"My go-to drink when I'm feeling down. I know it's a little out of season, but you did say fattening and sweet."

She picked up her mug for a sip. "Ooooh, it has a kick. I like it."

Fuck, his heart just flipped. He needed to stop that right now. Except his heart had other ideas. As a proper gentleman should, he pulled out a chair so Gillian could sit. She did and found herself with a lap full of cat before he could push her closer to the table.

"Knock it off." He pulled the cat off of her. "Sorry, I admit it, they're spoiled rotten."

"They're so cuddly. I'm jealous. I can't have pets myself. The manager at my complex has so many restrictions, and I always want more than I can afford. You're lucky: three cats, three tanks of fish, and gerbils all to yourself."

He sat adjacent to her so they could talk easily, but far enough away so he wouldn't crowd her. "They do keep me on my toes, but like I said, the gerbils aren't permanent. At least I hope not."

"Well, you can't snuggle them like you would a cat, but you have quite a city in that spare bedroom for supposedly temporary pets."

He had custom built a series of tunnel cages along with spinning wheels. Alek kept him supplied with plenty of cardboard boxes for the gerbils to chew. "I can't help it. I feel sorry for them being locked up all day, every day. I wanted to keep them entertained as best I could. It's cleaning the cages that gets tiresome after a while. And heaven forbid the cats break open the cages one day."

"That would turn into a track and field event," she giggled, before scooping up a glob of salsa onto a chip and into her mouth, chasing it with a gulp of hot chocolate.

Good Lord, he was going to die if she kept acting adorable like that. "Yeah, I guess it would."

"So, what's our next move?"

Maybe he shouldn't have had vodka this early in the day, because his body had an automatic and inappropriate response. "Move?"

"The bodies?" She looked at him as if his eyebrows had grown together. "We need to figure out why they were on the ship."

Well, that killed his libido right quick. "We don't do anything. The police can handle it."

Wrong answer from the way she shook her head. "No, we have to do something. *I* have to do something. I found them; I can't let this go. The police are tied up with the bombing downtown. They'll just put the bodies on ice. What if there's another attack? They might never get to the bottom of this because there will always be anti-Alts who want us dead."

He didn't like this turn of conversation. T-CASS might assist the police if a crime was committed by an Alt, but it wasn't part of their mission. "Let's not get paranoid. Yes, the police are dealing with the bombing and T-CASS is helping. I'm on medical leave, so I can't get involved with that."

"Exactly!" She slammed a hand down on the table. "We have the time. We can figure this out and find whoever did this."

"*I'm* supposed to lay low. I'm also not a detective. I wouldn't know where to start."

"The crew. T-CASS would have list of all of the crew

members by now. We can at least start looking into their backgrounds, see if we can spot anything suspicious."

"And I repeat: I'm not an investigator. That's Nik's realm."

She stared at him, just like his cats did when they were laying on the guilt trip—big, round, gold eyes, pleading with him to help.

Never let it be said that he wasn't a sucker. Maybe that was why he continued to work for T-CASS? He was an adult, so it wasn't like his mother could force him to stay if he didn't want to, and sometimes he regretted not following through on any of his other dreams. At one time he'd considered veterinarian school, but the program's demands on his time would mean leaving T-CASS for good.

But he loved what he did, even if it meant putting his dream aside. The only sacrifice he hadn't made was giving up his free time for a relationship. He didn't want one and didn't need one. "One and done" was his motto. Give the woman a taste and tickle, then move on because they might start to want more, and he had no time for that nonsense.

He had seen what serious relationships had done to his mother, at least until she met Thomas. Though his own father had found happiness with his stepmother, he just couldn't see putting that much energy into finding the right person. He had too much on his plate already.

Still, those wide gold eyes pinned him to his chair, so he relented. "All right. Let's see what we can do from here. I'm not contacting Nik, so we'll have to check this out on our own."

"Deal." She popped another chip into her mouth and pulled out her phone. "Let's log into the reports database and see if we can get that list of the entire Star Haven delegation and the cargo ship's crew."

This was not how he planned to spend the afternoon, but he had a tablet charging on the corner of an end table. He snagged that and logged into the T-CASS's computer system. "I also have the list of missing Alts provided by the Newcomers. What am I looking for?"

Gillian shrugged. "Connections to shipping, sailing, water. I don't know. We're assuming they boarded in Star Haven, but even for a relatively short trip, you'd need someone on the ship to sneak you on and off without the entire crew noticing."

"Unless one of them was an Alt that could accomplish the same thing with their ability." His father, Spook, could turn invisible, so it wasn't out of the realm of possibility that one of the victims could sneak the group on board with no one the wiser. He opened tabs to other social media sites and started plugging in names. Out of the corner of his eye, he could see Gillian nibbling while she poked at her phone. "Yeah, but they would still need to have experience with cargo ships in general, or have blueprints, at least to know where they could hide. And they'd need shift schedules to avoid getting caught. Not to mention having an ability that would open the hatch to the hold and close it again without attracting attention."

All good points. "Okay, let's do this."

Four hours and three boxes of popcorn and two more mugs of hot chocolate later, they had a list of two women and one man who might have some connection to the cargo ship, or knew someone who might have a connection, or might have sailed once across Mystic Bay.

"I'm calling it for the day." Evan blanked the screen on his tablet.

Gillian looked up from her phone, her fingers scratching the scruff of Kea's neck. "What? Why?"

"Because we're spinning our wheels here. There's only so much we can find out by typing names into a browser." Evan twisted in the chair so he could face Gillian. "Look, it's late. The sun's almost set. Unless my mom calls for a family meeting, I'm done. I'll take you home first."

Gillian pouted, her bottom lip inviting him to take a taste.

"Your cats will miss me." She pulled Crete to her chest for a snuggle. Lucky cat.

"He's still hoping for some tuna."

She kissed the cat before lowering him to the floor. "Maybe we can try again tomorrow?"

The hopeful look on her face caved whatever resistance he might have had. He couldn't tell her "no." "Sure. Where do you live?"

"Not far. Carousel Apartments, down the street from the seaquarium. I'm going to use your bathroom before we leave."

He watched her head back toward the spare bedroom, the cats in tow. If any other woman found herself in close proximity of his bedroom, there would be no leaving until morning, and that pulled his drawstrings too tight.

He stacked the plates using his ability, floating them toward the kitchen. Same with the glasses. He'd drop Gillian off, then head to a club. Maybe Champions, or perhaps Maxim's. He'd find someone to keep him company tonight, anyone, to distract him from all of these messy emotions complicating his life.

With the plates balanced on air, he opened the dish washer. Why did it smell like something was burning? Why was it suddenly so hot?

Heat, pain—the explosion hit him again. The plates crashed to the floor, but the sound of his body hitting the deck drowned out all other noise. The flames set his clothes on fire; his skin turned red, bubbling and crinkling.

"Evan!"

Someone called his name. Was it his mother? Lifting him out of the inferno, careful not to break him any more than he'd already been broken. Something snapped, like a balloon. He dug the heels of his hands into his eyes.

Make it stop. Make the burning stop.

He heard water running, cool and calming, making the fire go away. Wet hands cupped his face, soothing the heat, banishing the nightmare.

"Evan. It's okay. You're going to be okay. Please. Give me your hands."

He pulled his hands away from his eyes, but the world was still blurry. Despite the confusion, he could see Gillian standing in front of him, touching him.

"I'm sorry," he said. "I, uh—"

"Had a flashback?"

"Yeah." He took a deep breath. "Whatever was burning set off a memory loop. I was back in the fire and couldn't escape."

Her thumbs rubbed his skin, slippery, but the effect soothed him.

"One of the burners on the stove was turned on high. That was what you smelled."

Half of his brain was still locked on his past pain. "I must have forgotten to turn it off when I melted the chocolate."

"Maybe." Gillian grabbed a hand towel, stuck it under the faucet before patting it against his forehead. "Or the cats could have turned it on."

They'd never done it before, but it wasn't out of the realm of possibility. "I guess. I didn't have it turned on high, or we would have smelled it all the way in the living room long before now.

"Look, I need a few minutes before I fly you home..." He dragged in a shaky breath. Before he could finish, Gillian leaned in and kissed him.

HE LOOKED SO sad and hurt, how could she not try to make him feel better? Except she hadn't planned to keep kissing him, or for him to return the favor. Now she knew how Evan managed to get his reputation. This boy could kiss, and kiss, and kiss until she opened her gills to breathe while she pushed her tongue into his mouth.

Without warning, he pulled away. She tried to follow his lips but noticed she had backed him against the refrigerator.

"Gillian, we can't be doing this." His hands found her shoulders, but he didn't push her away.

"Because of T-CASS?" She couldn't think of another answer but talking to him gave her an excuse to step away from his tempting lips, while still remaining close enough to touch him.

"Because, well, I thought you preferred women."

That wasn't the reason; it was just a convenient excuse. Typical guy, thinking she couldn't want him because she'd hadn't dated a man since high school. "I prefer to have someone who wants me, regardless."

The more they talked, the more her doubts crept in. Did she want to become just another one of Evan's cast-offs?

What the hell? You've already been dumped by so many others, what's one more?

Her conscience had a point, but poor Evan still looked unsure.

"I could sleep with you so easily right now," he said, panting a little, his breath tickling her ear. "You look so damn good to me, and I've been thinking about what it would take to make you scream my name all afternoon. But I won't do this if you think you'll have regrets in the morning. I don't want to sleep with you and wake up thinking I took advantage of you. You're hurting just as much as I am."

No one had ever given her that much consideration before they slept with her. It was certainly more than the son of a bitch she'd dated in high school. Not that all of her relationships had ended as abruptly as that one, but at least Evan wasn't promising more than a single night of pure pleasure. She wanted to feel good. She needed this.

"I think I'm the one taking advantage of you."

His eyes skimmed her face, as if looking for a clue that she didn't really mean it. Finding nothing, because she meant what she said, he stepped back into her personal space. "In that case, carry on."

And she did. Just like at the pier, she picked him up, hauled him into a fireman's carry, and marched off to his bedroom.

"Oh, my." The room looked like the aquarium where she worked. She'd seen the three fish tanks in the living room, but he had two more in his bedroom. These tanks were ten gallons each and located far enough apart as to not strain the structure of the apartment. She couldn't help but check out the one nearest his bed.

"Five glofish tetras, three platies, two dwarf plecos, and a betta. How often do you change the water? Do you dechlorinate it first?"

"Fifty percent changed from every tank each week. All the water is dechlorinated."

"You have time for all of that?"

"I trained a couple of kids to come in three times a week to look after the menagerie. They're very good at keeping the tanks clean."

The thermometer read a balmy seventy-eight degrees. "Do you vary the temperatures?"

"No, I don't. Um, could you put me down now?"

Oooops. Maybe she still had some vodka in her. She flopped him onto his back, noting that the bed was king sized. It would have to be for a guy as big as Evan. He laughed as his head hit the pillow but managed to remove his shirt and kick off his shoes. She wandered back over to the fish tank while she stripped off her shirt.

"Tetras and guppies. Are all of your fish rescues too?" She watched the schools dart back and forth across the tank, weaving easily through the ferns and hornwort.

The lights dimmed, which didn't do much for her, as her eyesight adjusted along with it.

"Yes. Sometimes folks will abandon their homes, leaving their pets behind. I'm careful about what fish I'll accept."

She turned back to Evan, who had the light controller in his hand and half of his body under the covers, hiding the more interesting parts. The rest of him looked toned and tanned, thick muscles she wanted to test against her own. For all of his Alt ability, he didn't have super strength like her. Could he wrestle with her and win? Maybe, maybe not. The challenge when she slept with someone, male or female, was making sure she didn't squeeze too hard, or move too fast, or get so far out of control that she hurt them.

Evan looked as if he could take it, but could he give it right back to her?

Wouldn't that be fun, sleeping with someone who could outmaneuver her without even trying. She slipped under the covers next to him. He rolled toward her, running a hand through her hair. She groaned.

"Yeah, I know, not the long, wavy style you're used to."

"Who said I needed long, wavy hair to get turned on?"

He continued the path down to the back of her neck, tickling her. She shivered when his fingers paused right at the edge of her hairline.

"Most of your dates have long, wavy hair. I read the papers. I know what you like."

"No, you don't. The papers have a certain type in mind and

that's who they photograph. If I date someone who doesn't look like the type that will sell papers, you'll never see them."

"Um, does that mean you've dated more women than even the papers report? How do you get any work done?"

"Is this one of those 'can't win for losing' questions?"

"Depends on whether or not it's my name you call while inside me."

"Well, in that case, I think we'd better stop talking. I might need another drink—"

They both chattered too much, so she rolled on top and kissed him again. His hand remained on the back of her head, keeping her lips in place. His tongue danced along her lips, teasing her with more to come. His other hand slipped down to one of her breasts...oh, yeah, right there. A past lover had once speculated that she was more sensitive than Norms because of her need to withstand the intense pressure of swimming in deep water. Maybe it was true, but she'd been offended by the unnecessary comment and cut that relationship off before she got any satisfaction.

If Evan thought anything about her body beyond the soft skin he massaged with such precision, he at least had the grace not to say so when he squirmed underneath her while he slipped off his own t-shirt. She followed suit, enjoying the feel of his jeans rubbing her between her straddled legs. She discarded her bra and decided she would be the one to divest him of his jeans.

First, she grabbed his hands, capturing them before they could move from her belly to her breasts. She forced them over his head. He got the picture without her having to give a command. He waited patiently while she unzipped his fly at the pace of a sea slug, her fingernails trailing behind the zipper. Despite the passive position, he did assist with the actual removal of said jeans by lifting his hips so she could slide them down his long legs.

His legs weren't the only things that were long.

She tossed her own clothes over a nearby chair and climbed back onto Evan, who still had his hands up over his head. She stretched out on top, her knee nudging him from below before straddling him. Her hands found his to bring them down. He tried to lace his fingers with hers, but he'd forgotten about the webbing between the lower part of her fingers. It made holding hands difficult, if not impossible.

Instead of making a big deal of it, he released her hand so he could kiss the tips of each finger. He avoided her gills when his lips trailed along her upper arm to reach her left breast, hardening her nipple. She rubbed herself against him, trying to speed up his actions, but so far, he avoided an obvious show of his desire.

He did desire her, though, or else why would he curl lower in her arms, his head against her breasts, while his hands trailed around her torso to find her backside, pulling her closer between his legs, which he widened to accommodate her. By now, his hardness started to show as well. About time. She found his mouth again, and he scorched her with a kiss that stole her sense of time. His hot mouth made her want to fall into him, over him, and never leave.

While he kissed her, he shifted under her, but she didn't notice until he flipped her onto her back.

"My turn." He drew her hands up over her head. Oh, she could break free, and he knew it, but the surge of power teased her control. She wanted this. It had been too long since anyone made her feel as if they wanted to make love to Gillian, not Gilly. Evan wanted her as herself, not as an Alt he could bang and brag about.

She played along, keeping her hands off his body, while he

slid down, finding all the sensitive spots, stopping to suck, tickle, and rub just long enough to make her crave him above anything else. She couldn't help herself and had to dig her own fingers into the mattress to stop herself from hauling him back up to her face so she could kiss him again.

The moan caught her unawares, the need for more friction growing by the second. He knew what she wanted, but she wasn't willing to wait any longer. So she sat up and grabbed him under his shoulders and pulled him up until he covered her body. He was ready for her too, but instead of giving in to her needs, he pressed a finger across her mouth. She almost bit him.

"Whoa, hang on. One second."

He wasn't teasing; at least she didn't think so. For a moment she waited while he rolled off of her. The sound of a drawer opening from the nightstand, followed by the crinkle of a packet, made her realize what he was up to. She had forgotten about that part and was grateful he had remembered.

"Ready?" He rolled back into place as if he'd never left.

Instead of answering, she kissed him again, sucking in his lower lip, then his upper lip. He dueled with her, teasing with a few nips of his own before he slid inside.

She rocked with him, keeping him secure between her legs. Her gills flared despite her breathing air; her hands gripped his shoulders, pushing and pulling as her pleasure rose with his. His hands found her breasts again, rubbing her nipples, adding to the sensation of need.

They moved in tandem until they broke through together, and she heard him call her name. His voice pushed her even higher and she rode the second wave as it washed over her. The moment stretched until she thought she could see her life forever like this with Evan. Her pleasure passed, replaced with a sense of comfort.

Evan lay on top of her, his breath in her ear. He pulled out and rolled to the side, his hands still touching her, massaging her stomach, her arms, wherever he could reach.

"You are amazing." His voice cut through the pleasant buzz in her head.

"You're not so bad yourself."

One of his fingers ran from her hip up her side, tickling her, then to her shoulder, and then toward her neck. He didn't try to touch her gills, but he wanted to. They all had wanted to.

"It's okay," she said. "Just on the outside, though, and don't try to hold them closed."

With all the gentleness of a feather, he traced the outer edge of one gill from under her earlobe toward the bottom of her chin.

"Soft." He pulled his finger away. "And you're not comfortable."

"It's like having someone touch the edge of your nostrils, I guess. Not quite a turn on, but not painful either."

He snuggled closer to her. Interesting. She hadn't figured he'd be the snuggling sort, which proved she shouldn't guess a guy's reaction by what she read in the papers. By this point, she'd figured he'd be in the shower and getting ready for a night on the town, desiring a new conquest.

"What are your plans for the rest of the night?" he asked.

She hadn't thought that far. She hadn't thought of much since she pulled the bodies from the bay. The dead faces from the bomb blast killed any thoughts of going another round with Evan.

"I want to know the identities of the people who died. We need to confirm that they were Alts escaping Star Haven. I want to know who was helping them."

"If they had help," he said, reminding her of his doubts.

Kea pushed the door to the bedroom open and leapt onto

the bed. Gillian reached out the scratch the cat's ears while Kea sniffed at the bedsheets.

"Probably hungry again." Evan stretched, rubbing his body against hers, tempting her to start all over again, but she couldn't forget the dead.

"Clearly, you starve your pets." She kissed Evan on the nose as he grunted his agreement, then rolled off the bed, careful not to dislodge the cat. She picked up her scattered clothes from the floor, shaking out her t-shirt. "Mind if I use your shower?"

"Why don't you use the one in the guest room and I'll use this one. Just remember not to trip over the gerbil motel and keep the door closed so the cats don't follow you. I started with thirty-six gerbils, but one escaped and..." he waved a hand at the cat.

Gillian glanced at the cat, stretched out next to Evan, looking perfectly innocent while it licked one of its paws. "I'll be careful."

4

EVAN WAITED until he heard the water running in the other shower before he rolled out of bed, abandoning Kea, who glared at the loss of her human pillow. Most of the women he brought home either left on their own or hung out until he had to leave for work. He didn't mind either way. Some of them were interesting enough for conversation, but either they got bored while he prepared food for his menagerie or had their own jobs to return to.

Gillian was different. Instead of wondering about everything else on his to do list, he was visualizing how each drop of water bounced off her hair and dripped down her back, curving along those same muscles that had gripped him tight and made him howl. With a twist, he readjusted the water temperature of his own shower.

Yep, a cold shower would prepare him for an evening with Gillian. If she wanted to investigate the dead Alts, he would help.

He suspected his mother would call him back to the estate once Thomas was discharged from the hospital, so Evan would bide his time until then. He waited until after his shower to check his messages, including a few from Alek. His twin had found Cory at headquarters.

He and Gillian would need a plan before they headed out, though. So, what would Nik do? His brother was the one who had a private investigator's license, and so did their father. Cory, as a former Star Haven cop, might have some training in that area, but he didn't want to bother his youngest brother. They had only just started talking again after a decade of silence. Best not to bother him with something tied to Star Haven.

A thought pinged just as he heard the door to his bedroom open again. He hadn't brought his clothes with him into the bathroom. This could be interesting.

He stepped out of the bathroom. Gillian stood in front of one of the fish tanks, watching the Tetras swim about, while Kea threaded herself around Gillian's legs. Gillian ignored the cat as Evan pulled clothes from a dresser drawer. He glanced in her direction to see if she would turn around to watch. Instead, he noticed his own reflection on the tank's glass. What a sneak. She watched him, but only in his reflection. Ha!

He didn't slow down, but he didn't rush either. Let her watch and enjoy the show. Next time, and there would be a next time, he might ask her for a show himself. Turnabout was fair play and all that.

She waited until he'd slipped his t-shirt over his head to talk to him. "I never expected you to be a fish type of guy. The cats don't surprise me, and you said the gerbils were temporary rescues, but fish?"

"Yeah, they're not exactly the cuddly sort, but I inherited a few from a neighbor who had to move, and I kept adding more as time went by. They're relaxing to watch, especially after a long day. I can just lie in bed, propped up on a couple of pillows, and watch them swim around with one of the cats curled next me."

Speaking of which, he picked up Kea as an excuse to get

closer to Gillian. They both petted the spoiled creature for a minute, not looking at each other.

What was Gillian thinking?

"What now?" she said. "Our list of names is short and we could still be completely wrong about a crew member sneaking the Alts on board."

So much for his hope that maybe she was thinking about him. "The survivors are staying at the hotel at the north end of the boardwalk. We could just go down there."

Gillian leaned closer, and Evan held his breath, hoping she was going to touch him and maybe rekindle their passion, but instead she pressed her lips to the top of the cat's head. The cat, of course, adored the attention and purred louder with an accusing look at Evan, as if to say, *Yeah, I'll tolerate her kisses because* you *certainly haven't kissed me all day, you bum.*

"Good idea," she said, while continuing to scratch the cat's ears, "but we don't know what we're looking for. I mean, a smuggler isn't going to just jump up and say, 'yeah, I'm trafficking Alts.'"

Evan thought about that for a minute while the cat yawned and stuck her nose into the crook of his arm. "I think we need to watch videos of the harbor attack. It'll give us a good look at the delegation and the ship's crew. We can observe their behaviors, look for someone who's not where they were supposed to be or who's acting odd."

"See if any of them have a tell, like poker players."

"Yes, that's it."

"Are you sure you want to?"

Evan stroked the cat's soft fur. Did he want to relive the experience of almost burning alive? "Not really, but we'll just fast forward through the part where I fall."

"Okay. Where do you want to do this?"

Evan set the cat back onto his bed, even as she protested

with a flick of her tail. "Living room. TV would be easier than the desktop."

It took a few minutes, but Evan managed to find enough footage on the news sites to cover most of the attack. Gillian handed him a bottle of beer, which he set down on the end table, shooing away Crete before he could knock it over.

"I'm ready." Gillian crossed her arms, her eyes on the screen, grim determination on her face.

Evan swallowed. She might be ready, but was he? The remote in his hand shook, the light tremor making it harder for him to hit the play button. He managed to do it, though, and—he hoped—without Gillian noticing.

The reporter took up most of the screen for the few minutes leading up to the Star Haven delegates leaving the ship, so Evan fast-forwarded through the babbling. As the delegates disembarked, he and Alek soared above the ship, but the camera focused on the delegates. Thunder City was used to seeing Alts. The real news was written on the faces of the delegates. Some of them looked to the sky, either fascinated or disgusted by Rumble and Roar's flight.

That was the beauty of Thunder City. He and his brother worked *with* the Norm longshoremen to remove the cargo.

"I doubt the interim mayor or any of the other city government officials would be smugglers," Gillian commented. "They're too high profile."

Evan agreed, but he couldn't turn away from the screen. As the seconds ticked by, he could feel a sense of dread creep over him. Heat that didn't exist plucked at the tips of his fingers and toes. When the first gunshot was fired, he jumped, his elbow knocking into the bottle. It teetered but didn't spill.

If Gillian noticed, she didn't say anything. "We still don't know who the gunman is, do we?"

Evan grabbed the bottle and took a long swig to force the

bile back down his throat. "No. Not yet. SWAT didn't find anyone on the upper floors of the warehouse."

The news stream shifted to an overhead view from one of the news choppers as everyone at the dock scattered. He caught a glimpse of himself and Alek, holding steady despite the chaos below. "Let me slow this down..." His hand shook, but he found the right buttons to change the video's speed.

The two groups split apart. The Thunder City delegates raced toward the parking lot while the Star Haven delegates ran back toward the cargo ship. All except one.

"Look at him." Gillian pointed to the screen. "He's protecting the Blood Surfer."

"Her name is Hannah." The name got stuck in his throat. Evan pushed back the fear escalating in his chest and watched the dark-haired man kept himself between the potential danger and Hannah. He expertly weaved his way through the rampaging crowd until he shoved Hannah into the arms of Dr. McNamara. It looked as if words were exchanged before he turned and ran back towards the cargo ship.

The ship exploded.

Evan jumped, even though he had known it would happen. Out of the corner of his eye, he saw Gillian turn to look at him, not at the screen. The debris from the ship hurled into the sky along with the smoke, the heat pounding his back, and the next thing he knew...

Gillian grabbed the remote out of his hand and turned off the screen. The image disappeared but the heat remained, his skin burning as he fell again into the fire. Gillian reach out to him, touching him, reminding him he wasn't alone.

"Breath through it," she whispered. "Deep breaths. Fill your lungs. I'll be right here."

He did as ordered but also scrunched his eyes, wrapping himself around her voice. He found a rhythm, which matched the one she created by rubbing his arm, nice and slow. The heat receded, the agony of bruised bones and burnt skin disappeared, and he found his whole self once again.

"Don't force it." Her mouth was close enough that the tickle of her breath caressed his ear.

Crete took the opportunity to jump on his lap.

"Oh, no you don't." Gillian wrapped an arm around Crete to pull him off, but Evan reached out to tug the cat back into place, stroking soft fur.

The cat settled down, which allowed Evan to relax even further. He found his center again and opened his eyes.

Gillian's face was right in front of him, so beautiful to him.

"Do you want me to call someone? Your brother? Your mom?"

He shook his head. The last thing he needed right now was family. The worst of the panic had passed; he would never have to watch the video again.

They had their target.

Gillian still leaned against him, so he kissed her. She indulged him, but instead of arousing him further, it relaxed him.

"You are amazing," he whispered.

She pulled away, looking confused. "Really? For kissing you?"

"For sticking around, for not panicking, for working with me instead of running away or calling for help."

She ran her fingers through his hair. "I wouldn't do anything unless you wanted me to, or if I thought you were going to hurt yourself or me."

"I'd rather die than hurt you."

He meant it. Maybe it was the heat of the moment, maybe it was the look of trust in her eyes—the irises now showing off their bright gold—but he knew that she meant more to him than he could have imagined. A few hours ago, he would have said this feeling wasn't possible. Now, he couldn't imagine not having Gillian in his life.

Still, he had to convince her. She already thought she knew him based on his reputation. He would have to prove her otherwise.

"Let's focus on the guy protecting Hannah." He pulled back, giving himself space to think. "He looked familiar, like I should know him, but I can't quite place a name with the face."

"Who would you know from Star Haven?" Gillian asked.

Good question. "I keep up with the news, but the anti-Alt organizations don't broadcast their memberships."

"This guy wouldn't be with the anti-Alts, not acting like he did, protecting an Alt. He just painted a huge target on his own back," Gillian said.

"Yeah, but he'd still need police or security training to have been included with the Star Haven delegation. Someone trusted him, or he wouldn't have been able to cross Mystic Bay for this operation."

Gillian frowned. "On the other hand, it's not like Star Haven has a lot of trusted police officers to choose from these days. The last T-CASS report I read said many of their police force had disappeared once Dane died. That's what started this whole clusterfuck in the first place."

So many pieces of the puzzle were missing. He only knew one Star Haven police officer—his brother, Cory, who was known as Scott Grey in Star Haven, and still used that name with everyone except his family. But Cory had a partner on the force—Juan Costenaro. Evan had never met the man, and only knew his name because Thomas had kept a close eye on Cory once he moved across the bay.

"Would you hand me that tablet over there?" He pointed at the end table on Gillian's side of the couch.

She reached over, unplugged the charger, and handed him

the tablet. With a couple of clicks, he pulled up an image of
Officer Costenaro from a news report involving the Left Fist riots
a few weeks ago.

"This is him." He handed the tablet to Gillian so she could
confirm what he saw.

"Yeah, that looks like him. Hair style's a little different, but
the face is the same. Who is he?" Gillian handed back the tablet.

Evan blanked the screen. "Cory's old partner on the Star
Haven police force."

"Does Cory know he's here?" Gillian asked. "Maybe Cory
could talk to him for us? He might be more cooperative if he's
questioned by someone he trusts."

Evan shook his head. "I don't want to bother my brother with
this just yet. He's got a lot on his mind right now with Hannah
and the Oversight Committee. Let's leave him be until we know
for sure this guy was smuggling Alts, or at least knew they were
hiding in the ship. We can do this on our own. If we run into
trouble, we can always call for backup."

He made his way toward the porch and slid open the doors,
using his foot to keep the cats inside. Gillian followed him.

"We'll land at Brooks' Deli mid-boardwalk. That way we
won't attract too much attention." He reached out for Gillian. No
particular reason, other than that he wanted her in his arms
when he launched. "Ready?"

She smiled. "Let's go."

He created the vortex and launched with her snug in his
arms.

GILLIAN KNEW Evan didn't need to hold her to fly her to the
hotel, but she didn't resist when he pulled her into his arms.
After so many months mourning her latest breakup, it felt good

to snuggle into someone's embrace, even if Evan only meant for this to last for the night. Sleeping with him hadn't been part of her plan, but he had seemed so distraught. His emotions mirrored her own, and she'd needed solace after the horror she found that afternoon. He must have needed it, too, but even if he hadn't, she wouldn't regret her night with him. She wouldn't allow herself to.

She wanted to do right by the dead, give them a measure of justice. Evan understood her need, even if he had slept with her for his own reasons. If what they had shared helped both of them, then so be it. He had the stronger connection to T-CASS than she did. T-CASS only called on her when the harbor or the bay was involved. She could do so much more, but she would also have to advocate for herself.

Right now, T-CASS wouldn't want her as a member if they knew how she really felt about Norms.

Evan won't want you, either.

That thought chilled her rage. Evan might think more of her than he had of his previous hook-ups, enough to help her with her quest, but in the end, he was a dedicated member of T-CASS and Catherine Blackwood's son. He wouldn't want to be with someone who didn't toe the line with his mother's philosophy.

They landed where Evan had planned, far enough away from the hotel to not make a scene in front of the Star Haven survivors who might not appreciate Alts showing off their abilities. They needed to be able to search for this Juan guy without distractions. No one else on the boardwalk looked at them twice without their uniforms. They were just a happy couple out for a stroll—at least she'd like to believe that was what everyone else would think until they saw her gills.

"Now what?" she asked. "Maybe we should have disguised ourselves? I could wear a scarf?"

Evan looked at her as if she'd just grown horns. "Alts don't wear masks in Thunder City. That flies in the face of everything my mother has been fighting for since before I was born."

"Yeah, but we're not here as Alts. We're here as detectives," Gillian pointed out.

"No. No masks, no scarves, no hats. We already landed far enough away so we don't cause a stir by making a display of our abilities. If the Star Haven delegates can't handle Alts walking up the steps to a hotel in our own city without causing a ruckus, that's on them."

Mixed emotions stirred in her gut. "What about the Captain? Aren't you supposed to be on medical leave?"

He winced, but didn't stop walking. "You let me handle my mother."

Her pride swelled because his words matched her own feelings. They shouldn't have to hide themselves anywhere, not just in Thunder City. That was why her parents chose to move here, instead of farther south. They chose a city where their daughter would have a better chance of living a happy life, instead of winding up imprisoned or dead just because she looked different.

Still, if they needed the cooperation of a Star Haven police officer, would approaching him as Alts really be the wise choice? Especially in front of the other Star Haven delegates and the ship's crew?

Gillian clutched Evan's hand as they walked along the boardwalk, which became wider with more ornate decorations as they approached the hotel's walk-through entrance. Guards at the entrance gave them a once over before a sharp nod. She suspected they recognized Evan's face, but only figured out who she was by her gills, which she flared for a second when their eyes rested on her a second too long. Maybe she should spend more time on land.

She would if Evan gave her a reason.

No matter how this ended, she could always dream of the few happy minutes they'd had walking together like a real couple.

Inside, the lights from the ceiling highlighted the fountain in the center of the lobby, an oblong pool with dolphins and swans carved into it. The white noise of the fountain masked the chatter of the other hotel occupants. Most of them sat in clumps on the thick chair cushions, heads bowed together, talking to one another, or scrolling through their phones.

Evan took her arm as the atmosphere shifted, tugging her toward a small shop selling overpriced souvenirs and sundries. Not everyone stared, but they all knew who Evan was, or at least identified them both as Alts. She couldn't help but flare her gills again in agitation. The suspicion mixed with violence rolled around the polished tile in waves.

"Maybe this wasn't such a good idea." She kept her voice low, her eyes on the shop's window display.

"I see him. He's sitting by himself, near the concierge desk." Evan turned away from the crowd and followed her lead by looking at the window himself. Gillian could see their target too, reflected in the glass. He wasn't in uniform, just jeans, tan shirt, and a hoodie.

"We can't approach him out in the open like this," she said. "If he's an ally, then we'll be outing him in front of everyone. What do we do next?"

"We wait, I guess. Maybe he'll go back to his room. We can follow, then maybe call the room? Ask him to meet us somewhere else?"

"Yeah, because that's real subtle." She didn't have any better ideas, though.

No one approached them, so they stood there for what felt like hours, but must have only been a few minutes. Evan leaned a shoulder on the glass window, fiddling with his phone. She leaned toward him, trying to appear interested in whatever appeared on the news stream. He clicked on an article, an update on the situation downtown.

"Twelve bombs. That's far too many to just take down a hospital," she said.

"Yeah. The killer that Mom flew into the atmosphere would have taken out the hospital, the clinic, and the rest of the block." Evan clicked out of the article, and over onto the next.

"He's moving." Gillian ran her hand up Evan's arm to stop him from following. "Give him a head start."

She watched the reflection again in the glass, the sound of the man's shoes tapping on the tile making it easier to track his location. Instead of heading toward the carpeted corridor leading to the first-floor rooms, or toward the elevators, he walked toward the back entrance that led to the boardwalk.

"All right." Gillian slipped an arm around Evan's waist, looking up at him as if he absorbed all of her attention. "Time to leave."

Evan tugged her in the opposite direction, running his fingers through her hair, making a show of returned affection. "Let's head out the front. We can circle around through one of the shops."

"Good idea." She stood on tiptoe to give him a quick kiss.

He placed his hand on the small of her back, his palm warming her, reminding her of his soft massages.

The glass door swished open. They turned left in unison, where a small art shop had its doors wide open. The sun had set over the bay, so she hoped the hotel's shadow made it too dark for anyone to track them.

The art shop's display included several large glass pieces, so she and Evan had to slow their pace as they wound their way through the store.

"Do you see him?" She couldn't; even with her superior

eyesight, which allowed her better night vision, she didn't see the cop anywhere.

"Let's head north. Maybe he went for a walk along the boardwalk. The delegates aren't under house arrest. They're just supposed to be available if investigators have more questions."

They walked in tandem, their slow rhythm matching the waves hitting the pylons below. A ferry chugged its way to the landing; the service had just restarted after the hostage situation two weeks ago.

The dock had a larger crowd gathered around. Gillian didn't recognize anyone waiting to board. Not surprising, since Star Haven only allowed Norms into their city, and would use biometrics at the other end to make sure no known Alts were trying to sneak across the border.

"I see him," Evan said. "Next building over, sitting on the bench near the menu sign."

Gillian saw him too. The cop had stopped in front of the cafe. It looked as if he'd already ordered a cup and was waiting for them.

They really did suck in the sneaking around department.

Evan doubled stepped a few times to walk ahead of her. To protect her? She hoped not, though the thought was sweet. She could protect herself—and Evan if need be.

Maybe they'd make a good team in a fight? She hoped they wouldn't have to find out tonight.

Juan didn't acknowledge them as they approached. He just sat there, sipping his coffee as if he had not a care in the world. She did notice that he'd chosen one of the few benches that didn't sit under an overhanging lamp, making it harder for folks with normal vision to see him.

"Juan Costenaro?" Evan asked.

"You wouldn't be following me if you didn't already know that."

He didn't sound angry, just stating a fact.

"I'm..."

"A Blackwood," Juan interrupted. "One of Scott's brothers."

Gillian had to think about the name change. Juan would have known Cory Blackwood as Scott Grey. The news media used both names since Scott/Cory had never stated which one he preferred. No one had been able to get close enough to him since this whole debacle had started.

"Evan Blackwood." Evan reached for her, pulling her closer. "Rumble."

Juan took another sip of his drink, not challenging them, but not giving them a friendly gesture either. "Even in Star Haven, we know who Rumble and Roar are."

Gillian decided not to waste time introducing herself. It was obvious he didn't recognize her and didn't care. "If you keep up with the news, then you must have heard by now that we found twenty-five dead bodies in the cargo ship."

The cop swallowed hard, his eyes down now instead of looking across the bay. "Yeah, I heard."

"They were in one of the holds," she continued. Evan remained silent, letting her interrogate this guy without interruption. "There was no reason for them to be there."

He said nothing and still wouldn't look at them.

"We suspect they were Alts. Alts who hadn't left Star Haven before the Alt ban went into effect. They were trying to escape."

"Can't blame them for that. Being an Alt in Star Haven could get you killed."

Gillian bit back a retort about how Alts weren't a threat. "Except why would they choose that cargo ship? A ship filled with Norms, including the acting mayor of Star Haven and his entourage. They're supporters of the Alt-ban. They would prefer to see Alts dead."

"True enough, but it's not like the Alts could just board any ferry without getting arrested. Taking a private ship across would cost money, a lot of money. They probably didn't have that kind of cash on them. If any of them had an ability that could get them across the bay safely, they would have already done it. If they could have called T-CASS without getting caught, they would have done it. The Star Haven police monitor all communications into and out of the city, looking for Alts. They were trapped and they knew it."

Any doubts Gillian had about this guy disappeared. He knew everything and he was going to tell them.

"They couldn't have gotten on board the ship without being seen," Evan said. "They would have needed help. Only someone who was either part of the crew, or part of the delegation, would have had access to the ship before everyone boarded. That someone would have had security clearance. It would have had to be someone the mayor trusted."

Costenaro crushed the paper cup in his fist. "Yeah. They would have needed help. They were trying to leave but had all of these excuses as to why they couldn't leave before the ban. I'm a cop, not an executioner. I got them on board, and another crew member managed to get them in the hold. We made sure they had food and water and... whatever else they needed for the journey. It was only going to take a few hours to cross. We'd wait until nightfall to get them out unseen. What did I care, as long as they were leaving and not creating a fuss?

Gillian couldn't stop her anger. "And now they're dead because no one knew they were down there except you and one of the crew, and they didn't have any abilities to keep themselves safe."

"Like I said, I'm not an executioner." Costenaro tossed the cup into the nearby garbage bin with more force than necessary. "I wanted to get them here to Thunder City and away from Star Haven. I didn't arrange all this just to get them killed."

"We know." Evan sat down next to Costenaro before Gillian could stop him. "We saw you on the video. You put yourself between Hannah and danger to keep her safe. You don't hate Alts, and you did your best to protect them."

"Don't get ahead of yourself," Costenaro snapped, but there wasn't a lot of heat behind the words. "Just because I didn't kill them myself doesn't mean I want to live in a city full of them."

And yet, he didn't move away from Evan. Costenaro sat next to an Alt as if it didn't matter. It didn't matter to Evan or to her, but for Costenaro to not try to inch away, to accept that Evan sat next to him, was a gauge of his commitment to a hateful law.

A piece of her own anger melted. She tried to grab it back, rekindle her outrage. There was power in outrage and yet, a large part of those burning embers snuffed out under Juan's unspoken pain at his failure.

She was about to question the cop further, when Evan stood and put his hand on her arm.

"We have trouble."

She turned around to face north. The ferry had docked, and the crowd had started boarding, but there was a smaller group that had worked its way behind the passengers, pushing their way through the tail end of the line. They had hoodies pulled low over their faces, and what looked like long batons in their hands, different sizes and shapes, but all for the same use.

"Do they really think those will work against us?" Gillian turned her back to the approaching mob, counting on Evan to watch her back.

"They're not after you two," Costenaro said. "They're after me. I met with Scott yesterday. I... didn't exactly try to hide it. They must have recognized him. They'll try to separate us, so they can get me alone."

"We won't let that happen." Evan motioned for Costenaro to stand. "I'll fly the three of us out of here."

"No!" Her voice was louder than she intended because she found her frustration as it roared back to life. "We can't let them get away with this. Not in *our* city. We need to send a message—Thunder City is for Alts. If Star Haven doesn't like it, then they can just go home. No one is forcing them to do this. If there is no attack, then there's no reason for the Thunder City police to arrest them."

She could see Evan reach for his comm, sending an emergency signal to headquarters. They would have backup soon if there were any Alts left for backup. After today—who knew?

"I have a better idea." Gillian kept her back to the attackers, still trying to preserve the illusion that gang could take them by surprise. "If you sweep them into the bay, I can create a riptide and drag them far enough away from shore to tire them out by the time they swim back. No one gets hurt."

The group started to separate, creating a single line across the boardwalk to prevent anyone from retreating back to the hotel.

"You're assuming they can swim. You can't rescue all of them at once if they can't. We need to think in worst-case scenarios. We can't afford another mass death."

Wind tickled her ankles. Evan was getting ready to launch them into the skies.

"I have my own backup. The dolphins won't let them drown."

"You can talk to dolphins?" Costenaro asked. He wasn't armed. His service weapon had probably been confiscated after the attack.

"No, but I play with them all the time. If one of the terrorists starts to slip under the surface and I don't notice, the dolphins will bump him back to the surface."

She hoped Evan bought into her reasoning. Killing the

group wasn't an option but letting them get away with menacing should have its own consequences.

"All right. I'll get Costenaro out of here after you're in the bay. Let's do th..."

Before he could finish, an explosion hit, smashing all three of them into the shop window.

5

"OH, FOR GOD'S SAKE." Evan rubbed the back of his head, checking for blood. Pure instinct saved the three of them. Since he'd started building the vortex before the anti-Alts lobbed a grenade at them, the wind had shoved the device just far enough away to prevent the explosion and shrapnel from hurting them, but not far enough away to avoid the shock wave shoving them against the store window. The window shattered, and he'd caught a few glass shards in his bare arms and back. He suspected Costenaro and Gillian had suffered the same.

"Where the hell did they get a grenade?" Gillian started to stand up.

"Who cares? Everyone stay down, play dead. Gillian, get ready to go swimming."

At least Costenaro had enough sense to listen to Evan. They lay still and let their attackers creep closer. A group of ferry passengers watched from the sun deck as the ferry launched. At least they'd have witnesses from Thunder City if they were lucky.

The attackers must have known this though because they

circled around, trying to shield the view of their three victims from the ferry passengers.

Evan stretched his fingers, waiting, watching, ready to act, while the bastards checked to make sure they were dead. Despite all his training, it would still take him a second or two to form another vortex. At least this particular store was closed for the evening, so there was no light from the interior and the nearest lanterns hanging from the poles lining the boardwalk had shattered. There was still a ton of debris around, most of it glass. He didn't care if he hit the anti-Alts with the shards, but if he hit Gillian or Costenaro, he could do more damage to them than the grenade had done.

Hurting Gillian, even with just a small nick, was unacceptable. Alek was the one who had the hot temper, but some days, Evan could match him on the heat scale. Today was one of those days.

With his anger growing, Evan had to fight to hold back on his assault until one of the anti-Alts was almost close enough to grab Gillian. Letting his emotions drive, he created a vortex in one second, and ramped it up to an F5 tornado. The anti-Alt lifted off the boardwalk, along with all his friends, his arms and legs flailing in the sudden loss of ground from under his feet. Before they could tumble free, Evan flung them over the departing ferry, picking up most of the glass shards with them, which cut through their clothes and into their skin. Let them feel the saltwater in their wounds. He was beyond caring at this point.

"Ready?" he shouted at Gillian.

"Yeah! Now! Do it!"

He redirected the vortex but with much more care. He lifted Gillian and carried her over the ferry, dropping her just to the north of where he had dumped the anti-Alts. He couldn't do anything for her now, except hope that her plan worked.

Thunder City didn't need more deaths. *He* didn't need an investigation that might reveal his waking nightmares before he could do something about them.

"Now what?" Costenaro whispered, still playing dead. His head was angled, so he'd seen what Evan had done. His voice was neutral, neither disgusted at being rescued by an Alt nor pleased.

Evan sat up, the glass stuck to his shirt, the tiny wounds drawing blood. "How do you feel about cats?"

"Cats?" Costenaro matched Evan, pushing himself up to a sitting position with care and a small wince.

Evan leaned forward, but his back burned as if on fire. *No. Not now. I can't lose control now.* He dug his palms into his eyes, breathing through the pain.

"You okay, man?"

Pain.

Flames.

No oxygen.

Dying.

Not fucking now.

The visions didn't stop just because he wanted them to. All he could do was ride it out. In the background, sirens wailed, faint, but getting closer. When he'd fallen onto the ship, he couldn't hear anything but the roar of the fire. The wail of sirens was enough to pull him out of his imagination and bring him back to reality. He dropped his hands from his eyes.

Had Costenaro moved closer to him? Hard to tell in the dark. What had he been trying to say before the wounds on his back triggered his memory? *Cats.* He had been warning Costenaro about his cats.

"I'm fine. Just trying to get debris out of my eyes." He shook his head as if trying to rid himself of more loose glass. "Look, Harbor Regional has been evacuated for the time being, and the other hospitals and clinics are overwhelmed from absorbing their patients. I can either take you to T-CASS headquarters for treatment, where you'll be surrounded by Alts, or I can take you to my apartment, where you'll be surrounded by cats. If both options freak you out, then we have a problem." Evan tucked his legs underneath him so he could stand without leaning on the window's frame, then offered a hand to Costenaro to help him to his feet.

Costenaro stared at his hand for a second as if it had claws, but then grabbed hold and let Evan haul him off the bed of glass. "What about your girlfriend?"

Juan didn't think he and Gillian were putting on an act before. Evan actually liked the idea that everyone could look at him and Gillian together and know how much he cared for her. Maybe they could see that she cared for him too?

"She'll be fine. Even if the anti-Alts are expert divers, their wet clothes will hamper any movement. Gillian joined them just to make sure they don't drown. Stand still—I'm going to get rid of some of this glass."

"They could still hurt her," Costenaro said, though he followed Evan's direction. "They probably had other weapons as well."

Costenaro was right, but Gillian would know if they had other weapons. At least he hoped she would.

"Weapons that won't react well to water. Still, Gillian will dive too far down for them to follow if she has to. She can breathe underwater, so she'll stay there until they tire themselves out."

Instead of filling his head with more worry, he built up his vortex again, this time around himself and Costenaro, creating a gentle vacuum. The vacuum pulled most of the loose glass off their clothes, but they would still have some embedded in their skin.

Costenaro looked him, then out to the bay. "She's really going to make sure they don't drown? After they damn near killed her? You?"

"That's the way T-CASS works. Gillian dislikes Norms the way you dislike Alts. But she'll do her job and keep them alive, if for no other reason than the paperwork triples if they die."

Costenaro rubbed the stubble of his chin. "I'll go with the cats. Bringing me into the heart of Alt territory isn't a good idea right now."

Baby steps were better than no steps at all. The wail of sirens drowned out anything else they might say. He wouldn't be surprised if Thunder City had called in Division Six as well as SWAT. Too many attacks in the harbor this past year would make anyone, never mind the police chief, paranoid.

"Okay, we'll make our statements, then I'll bring you home."

Easier said than done. While the EMTs picked glass out of their skin and bandaged their bloody nicks, Evan's focus was stretched in three different directions: making sure his own report was as accurate as possible, keeping himself close to Costenaro, and watching the bay in hope of a glimpse of Gillian. He emphasized the need for the police to find her. The incident commander called in a request for a helicopter. They would also send a boat to rescue, and arrest, the anti-Alts.

Even though Costenaro kept his own report unbiased, Evan couldn't say the guy sounded all that enthusiastic about having his ass saved by Alts. It could have been shock over the attack, but perhaps it was an anti-Alt whose worldview was being challenged by reality?

One of the benefits of being a member of T-CASS, and maybe of being Captain Spectacular's son, was that the police didn't argue with him when he said he would take Costenaro to his apartment. His mom had inspected the building Evan had chosen, and Thomas had installed extra security that he routinely inspected. His apartment was as secure as T-CASS headquarters and the Blackwood family estate. The police knew that Costenaro would be as safe there.

The helicopter the police had promised flew overhead, the heavy rotors drowning out everyone's voice for a minute. Gillian would be in good hands if they found her. The anti-Alts—they would wish they had drowned.

The incident commander had walked away, so Evan made one last request to one of the rookie police officers. He passed along the request to his senior partner, who looked at Evan, then at Costenaro, and nodded his head.

"The car is parked a few store fronts down." The rookie stood closer to Evan than Costenaro. "Can you walk there safely?"

Costenaro gave Evan a raised eyebrow.

"If you want to fly, we can, but I figured you'd prefer to be driven."

"You got that right. Uh, thanks for giving me the option."

They followed the rookie through the tiny side ally between stores leading to the parking lot. Both of them winced as they walked down the steps; the bandages wrapped around their legs weren't doing them any favors. No lights or sirens, but the rookie got them back to Evan's building in under fifteen minutes. Another five passed, and Evan unlocked his front door, his foot ready to hold back the tide of outraged fur balls.

"Back up, Crete. C'mon, I have a guest. Let him through."

The cats ignored him, which was par for the course, but Evan managed to get Costenaro inside without being molested.

"There's food and drinks in the fridge, so help yourself. Television is all yours, too. There's three bedrooms down the hall; mine's on the left. You can use either one of the other two, but the farther one has a cage full of gerbils."

"Are you going to head back to the harbor?" Costenaro

reached down to pull Kea into his arms before she could climb him like an oak tree.

Evan sighed. "Yeah, I'll join the helicopter flying over the bay, not that I can do much good in the dark. My moth...I mean Captain Spectacular..."

"I know who your mother is." Costenaro kept his eyes on the cat, now content with having her ears scratched.

"Right. She has better night vision, but she's still at the hospital with my stepfather. If I can get Seeker to go with me, he'll be able to see through the water from above."

He was babbling, not sure how much Costenaro cared about how T-CASS operated. The cop continued to pet Kea for another minute.

"You guys really have a lock on this city," he said finally.

Evan shrugged. "We want to be safe, just like Norms. By contributing the safety of Thunder City, Norms can see us as allies instead of enemies trying to take over."

Costenaro looked up at him, his face neutral. "You better get going. And when you find your girlfriend..."

"Gillian."

"Yeah, when you find her, tell her I said thanks."

Evan nodded, and left Costenaro in the living room while he changed into his T-CASS uniform. Approved operation or not, his suit had safety features he would need for night flying. At this point, half the city would know that he'd been healed by Hannah. By tomorrow everyone would know. He might even wind up in jail alongside Hannah and Cory, but he was okay with that as long as he knew Gillian was safe.

When he returned, Costenaro was sitting on the sofa with a beer in one hand and Kea in his lap. The TV was turned on to one of the Thunder City twenty-four-hour news stations. Evan noted that he hadn't selected a Star Haven station.

He left the apartment via the porch this time, using his foot to keep Mykonos and Crete inside. He tapped the navigational lights—green on his right shoulder and red on his left, white on his lower back, just like an aircraft—so that the helicopter would know he was there. He also needed his night vision goggles so he could gauge how close he was to the helicopter and not knock it askew with his vortex. He didn't know if Costenaro watched his preparation or not, but he couldn't wait any longer. Gillian was depending on him to find the anti-Alts before they could do more damage.

He needed to find her to tell her how much he loved her.

He still wasn't sure what her response would be.

WITHOUT EVAN NEXT TO HER, Gillian's flight over Mystic Bay wasn't her most graceful moment. At the last second, she managed to stop tumbling long enough to dive head-first into the bay. Opening her gills gave her a sense of homecoming, even as the cold water enveloped her, welcoming her back. She belonged in the bay more than she belonged on the surface. At least that's what she had always told herself.

Her heart twinged. Evan lived on the surface. He had no ability to breathe in her world. If she wanted more from him, she would have lived more on the surface than in the bay.

Don't be stupid. Evan's a nice guy, dedicated to Thunder City, but he's not going to change his lifestyle for you. Why would he? What kind of trust fund playboy wants to spend his life with a woman who's half-human, half-fish?

She dove farther down on that thought. Regardless of how she felt, she had a job to do. Keep the anti-Alts from drowning so they could be brought to justice. They had to have known they wouldn't succeed. It took a certain sick mindset to sacrifice your freedom to kill off a couple of Alts.

Well, okay. Evan was a huge target, being the son of Captain Spectacular. Killing him would be a badge of pride for a determined anti-Alt. She doubted the anti-Alts even knew who she was, even if they saw her gills.

Seven pairs of legs thrashed above her as a small wave swept them closer toward the ferry. No reason for her to engage the bastards; she could just float below them far enough to observe. It gave her time to shed her civilian clothes so she could move around unrestricted. Her uniform would have at least acted like a wetsuit, but no point in regretting her decision to wear civvies now. She'd stay underwater to avoid giving the anti-Alts a free peep show.

Something poked her from behind. It was the young dolphin from the pod she often played with out near the Lazy Eight islands. She checked and saw that there were a few more in the background. The thrashing must have caught their attention, waking them if they'd been asleep. This dolphin had her colorful scarf draped around his pectoral fin.

He wanted to play, but she couldn't. One of the anti-Alts started to slip below the surface. If they'd had any sense, they would have shed their own clothes.

Gillian swam away from the dolphin until the anti-Alt was directly above her. She didn't want to touch the son of a bitch, so she sent a high-powered thrust of water upwards, pushing him higher. One of his buddies grabbed his arm to keep him afloat. Whatever.

As soon as she turned back to the pod, she saw a nightmare unravel as the dolphins started circling the group, trying to do her job and keep the anti-Alts alive. The dummies started to thrash harder.

No help for it; she had to surface to calm everyone down before someone got hurt. She still kept her distance though, and her chest below the surface.

"Shark! Shark!"

They saw the pod's dorsal fins and thought they were sharks. *Morons*. Sharks almost never wandered into Mystic Bay. The last attack she knew of had been over a century ago and the story was suspect. The more the anti-Alts panicked, the more likely they would drown.

She swam over to the nearest idiot. It took her a second to switch from water breathing to air, but she managed to grab his flailing arm.

"They're dolphins, not sharks. Calm down. You're going to drown."

She almost got an elbow in the face for her efforts. The anti-Alt's panic slowed, but she kept her grip tight on his arm.

"If I let go, will you be able to float for a few more minutes?"

He probably couldn't see her in the dark. In the background, over the sound of screaming and ocean waves, she could hear the *whoop-whoop* of what she hoped was a police rescue helicopter. The anti-Alt squirmed in her grip, but she refused to let go. Who knew what crazy thing he would do next?

She found out faster than she would have figured. With his free hand, he pulled something small and round from under his jacket. His thumb flicked a pin.

Another grenade.

"Die, freak!"

To her horror, he pulled her closer, the grenade in between them. He was willing to die if he could take her with him. Gillian had no time to think, no time to breathe. The countdown began. She squeezed the bastard's hand, breaking his wrist, and tried to grab the grenade, but her strength wasn't as strong as his hate. He managed to toss the grenade at the dolphins.

5...

White-hot rage overtook her good sense. What to do? In the background, the rhythm of the helicopter's rotors grew louder. If she forced the grenade higher, out of the water, she risked hitting the helicopter.

4...

Damn the anti-Alts and damn T-CASS regulations along with them for making her try to save them. She closed her throat, opened her gills, and dove under the anti-Alt. She gathered a vortex of water to propel the grenade lower and lower and lower. Unlike Evan in the air, water had far more weight and to keep the pressure up and the pathway down, she had to follow the grenade.

3...

Oh, no. No. *No!* One of the dolphins had followed her. The one with the scarf. He thought this was another game, but Gillian couldn't stop to distract him. She had to keep pushing.

2...

The dolphin shot past her, eager to get to his prize before she did.

1...

The explosion disrupted her vortex, the wave knocking her of course. Sharp pain exploded from her legs and stomach. She covered her face and neck with her bare arms as more shrapnel pummeled her forearms, but that didn't stop a fragment from slamming into her forehead.

The water filled with blood. Evan would find her body before she could tell him she loved him.

That was her last thought before she passed out.

6

EVAN HAD ROCKETED himself faster than usual, keeping low so he could use the lights of the city to guide his way. This debacle was caused by a non-sanctioned T-CASS operation. He had to remember that.

In a quarter of the time it had taken the rookie to drive him and Costenaro to his apartment, Evan was flying over the boardwalk. The ferry had stopped before reaching the mouth of the bay, perhaps ordered to because of the witnesses on deck. He found the helicopter with the searchlight, but no Gillian or anti-Alts. This was the general area he had aimed for. He dove into the spotlight, his goggles protecting his eyes, to make certain the helicopter occupants knew he was there, then moved farther away so his vortex wouldn't interfere with the copter's flight. The helicopter wobbled a little, acknowledging his presence.

His comm vibrated, followed by a chime in his ear. Evan activated the mic near his mouth.

"Welcome to the party, Rumble."

"What's the status?" He moved even farther away from the copter, so his voice wasn't completely drowned out by the noise of the rotors. He was surprised that they hadn't already found Gillian and the anti-Alts. They must have circled this area a number of times while he was getting Costenaro settled. He was certain these were the right coordinates.

"Nothing so far. We're seeing a lot of marine life, but nothing else."

"Gillian wouldn't have drowned. And she wouldn't have let the anti-Alts drown." At least he hoped so. His worry ratcheted from his stomach to his heart.

"We'll find her, Rumble. We won't stop looking until we do."

Evan peered farther across the bay, the last of the dark blue horizon slipping into midnight black. "Let's widen the search. Maybe I overshot my target. I wasn't exactly steady on my feet when I sent them flying."

The helicopter propelled forward with Evan flying in tandem. Eventually, the helicopter would have to refuel, but Evan vowed to fly all night, and all the next day. He wouldn't stop flying until he found Gillian.

He had expected to find her in minutes, but the minutes dragged out into an hour. Tossing seven Norms into the air might have thrown off his sense of how much propulsion he needed to generate to get them over the ferry and into open water, but he'd been more careful with Gillian. He had deliberately propelled her beyond the anti-Alts. She wouldn't have a problem swimming toward them if she had to.

Unless she had been more injured than they'd thought by the grenade. Even now he could feel his back throb in time with his heartbeat as blood coagulated against the bandages. Maybe Gillian had internal injuries? She was stronger than the average human, had the ability to withstand a hail of exploding debris, but she wasn't Captain Spectacular. Bullets could harm her, though not as badly as they might a normal human. Why hadn't he stopped to examine her before he tossed her into the bay?

What the hell kind of guy doesn't even check to see if his teammate, never mind his girlfriend, has internal injuries before throwing her back into battle?

His nightmare scenario grew worse every minute he couldn't find Gillian. He signaled the helicopter, indicating that he was breaking away to search on his own. He adjusted his goggles to compensate, and activated his own much smaller search light on his uniform. The extra light didn't help much, but it was better than nothing.

Instead of roaming the area where Gillian was supposed to be, he made concentric circles around the target area. Two police boats joined the search, disrupting his pattern, but he still welcomed the extra eyes.

His comm chimed again.

"We found the anti-Alts. Head back to us, we've got them in the spotlight."

"Gillian?" Evan asked, hoping against the tightness pulling his lungs into a sick twist.

There was a long pause. "Nothing. We haven't found her yet."

Evan wanted to shout, "keep looking," but he knew the police would have to disarm the anti-Alts before pulling them out of the water and resuming their search.

Three circles later, he noticed another break in the waves. Dorsal fins skimmed the surface, all moving against the waves and keeping together. Evan wracked his memory, trying to remember what little he knew about dolphins. This wasn't their normal sleeping behavior.

He flew closer to examine the pod, and then he saw her.

Gillian, right in the center of the dolphins, floating her back, not moving.

"I found her," he shouted into his comm. "She's unconscious, surrounded by dolphins. I'm flying right above her. I'll bring her to you."

It would take a hell of a lot of concentration to split his focus and create a second vortex under her.

"We're redirecting the second boat to you," the voice in his ear said.

Evan started to shout that he would lift her out of the water and rocket her to the nearest hospital, but he didn't. Just as he tried to create the second vortex, his nightmare poked at him. He froze.

Explosion.

Heat.

Alek.

Falling.

Alek.

Burning.

Pushing oxygen away.

Don't stop.

Can't breathe.

Don't think.

Just don't stop.

He couldn't move. Below him, Gillian floated, but in his mind's eye, she was surrounded by flames.

Stop the flames.

No, stop imagining them.

Evan still couldn't move. All he could do was watch as the rescuers from the second boat dove into the bay to help Gillian, while his nightmare played over and over again through his mind.

As soon as they hauled her into the boat, Evan managed to douse the nightmare flames. He landed on the boat as close as he dared without interfering with the professionals. He could see the shrapnel sticking out of Gillian's forehead, the blood flowing freely along her hairline, down her neck, pooling around her gills.

She gagged on the blood, her gills flaring for a brief moment, then closing. One of the rescuers shouted she wasn't breathing, but then her chest lifted as her mouth opened, sucking in air, the sound loud and painful.

Evan followed the boat as it sped back toward the harbor. He could have gotten her there so much faster, but the phantom heat, the sense of choking on nonexistent smoke, wouldn't leave him alone. As soon as the boat was secured, the divers lifted Gillian onto the dock, Evan following them.

Gillian hated the surface. He knew that but sending her back into the bay wasn't an option. She couldn't heal there. Not from these injuries.

She couldn't heal herself, but Evan knew who could.

That thought died almost as fast as he thought it. He wouldn't pull Hannah into this situation unless he had no other choice. If he had to choose between obeying the law and saving Gillian, Gillian would win every time. Hannah would understand. He didn't give a damn about the consequences.

Almost as if she knew what he was thinking, Gillian's eyes fluttered open. She looked around until she saw him. When she did, she held out her hand, which he took into his own and pulled close to his body, pouring all of his love into their connection. Could she feel it? Did she know how much he cared? His thumbs rubbed her knuckles in an attempt to warm her body, to show her what she meant to him.

"They killed him," she whispered.

What the hell had happened? He was careful to only send the anti-Alts and Gillian into the bay. Gillian wouldn't have let an anti-Alt die, no matter how much she hated them. He had to believe that. "Who? Costenaro? He's fine. He's in my apartment."

Tears formed in her eyes, spilling down her temples, mixing with the blood. No, it wasn't Costenaro who caused these tears.

"Who did they kill?" he asked.

She started crying more. One of the officers started to get her ready to lift into the ambulance, but Gillian clung to Evan's hand.

"I tried so hard." Her voice wavered, the heartbreak digging deeper and upending the last shred his own emotional equilibrium.

He had tried too, the container, the searing heat, falling, Alek watching, unable to help...

No! He closed his eyes and pushed back, shutting down everything else except Gillian's voice. Just Gillian. Only her and no one else. Not the other squad members, not the EMTs, not the police officers.

"One of them dropped a grenade. I pushed it far enough away so it wouldn't hurt the other anti-Alts, but the dolphin swam past me. He thought it was a game. I couldn't stop him in time."

Evan leaned down, careful to avoid her forehead. The shard of metal had been removed; the wound dressed to prevent infection. Instead, he pressed his cheek to hers, his eyes closed with his own helplessness. "I'm so sorry."

Behind him he heard one of the EMTs. "She's ready. We have an ambulance waiting in the parking lot."

Evan hated letting go of Gillian, but he couldn't ignore the EMTs waiting to lift her into the ambulance. They couldn't do their job with him hanging onto her. It took Evan almost a minute to break free out of his reverie, to look at the officer addressing him. How much time had passed?

"I can fly her to a hospital." He didn't need to leave his numb cocoon to generate another pillow under Gillian. Once he had her above the height of the stores lining the boardwalk, he'd fly her to...no wait, Harbor Regional wasn't available. He'd have to take her to the Fargrounds Medical Center, where Catherine waited on Thomas. He knew that. How could he have forgotten that?

"I don't think that's a good idea." The EMTs ignored him, and moved Gillian away from Evan. Another officer addressed him —a woman who stood close to Evan. Too close. If Evan launched with Gillian, he'd take the officer with him.

"I can take care of her." The words poured from his mouth without thought.

The officer walked around him, so she blocked his view of Gillian. "I know you can, but I must insist you ride in the ambulance. She's stable; she'll ride just fine. You need someone to care for you."

What did the officer see that Evan couldn't? Maybe the numbness was too obvious for even him to hide. Evan licked his lips, chapped from the bay air. "You're right."

The officer signaled the EMTs to continue. Soon enough, Gillian was inside the ambulance with Evan seated next to her, her hand back in his, his hold gentle against the webbing between her fingers. He didn't want to feel anything else except her.

It took twice as long to get Gillian to the hospital. Evan shifted his position more than once so he wouldn't interfere with the EMTs, but never let go of her hand. She didn't say anything. Her eyes were glassy, shifting between him and ambulance's roof, as if not seeing anything. He wished he could do the same as his nightmare started to repeat again.

The EMTs transferred Gillian from the ambulance and into the hospital with no assistance from Evan. His head said he should at least offer to help. His heavy heart kept his hand tight around Gillian's until a nurse the size of a linebacker in blue scrubs gently, but firmly, directed him to the waiting room.

Again, Evan's head told him to argue, but his heart let his hand slip away from Gillian's, knowing by instinct alone that this was for the best. Her eyes closed as his hand left hers, the medications pumped into her system sending her to sleep.

At least half a dozen people sat in the not quite comfortable chairs and battered sofas scattered around the waiting room. He found an empty seat in the middle of the room near a small table that offered old print magazines and few coloring books. Off in a corner, a coffee maker gurgled. If anyone recognized him, they said nothing. Or, maybe they did talk to him, but he didn't notice.

He let the nightmare envelope him again, the horrifying memory splashing over his brain like a wave. Heat, fall, pain, push, repeat.

He had no idea how long he'd been sitting there when a shadow fell over him. He tried to ignore whoever it was that had invaded his personal space, but the shape of the shadow appeared familiar. He looked up to see his mother standing there. Of course, she would be here, waiting by Thomas's side for him to recover from surgery.

She said nothing to Evan, and he said nothing to her. Her face was expressionless, which Evan knew from experience was how she looked when she didn't know what to do with her sons. They both waited a beat, then three. Finally, she held out her arms to him.

Evan stood. He'd towered over his mother since his fifteenth birthday, but height didn't matter now. He lowered his head onto her shoulder and cried.

AT FIRST, Gillian fought the rough seaweed entangling her. She struggled to breathe, seaweed entangling her gills, forcing her to struggle for oxygen. If she didn't tear herself loose or breach the surface of the bay, she would drown. Why was she even in

Mystic Bay in the first place? Had she been called in for an operation? She couldn't remember. The last thing she remembered was...

Rumble. Where was Evan? Gillian struggled again, her violence doing little to unwrap the seaweed. More clamped around her, restricting her ability to swim. She had to swim. She had to find Evan. He would help her. They needed to save...

Her eyes opened, though she hadn't realized they'd been closed. Harsh fluorescent light, not the searchlights, brought tears to her eyes. Hospital sheets, not seaweed, were wrapped around her body. Her lower half because a neck brace clamped around her neck so she *had* to use her nose to breathe. She clawed at it and kicked her feet, struggling to free herself.

"She's awake!" A flurry of activity surrounded her. Blurs of blue floated into her peripheral vision, too harsh for the bay and not dark enough for a dolphin.

The dolphin pod...her friend with the scarf...the grenade. Oh, God, she hadn't pushed it far enough away.

"Gilly? Gilly, stop fighting."

The woman used her moniker, enraging her even further. She was more than her gills, more than an Alt who could breathe under water, damn it. A door slammed nearby.

"Gillian. Relax, sweetheart. I'm here. We're trying to help you."

She could smell Evan before she could see him, the scent of dried bay water and fear. Her eyes still burned from the bright light. There was so much of it, how could anyone see?

Evan's face blocked the light, hovering over her. "Gillian, please. We need you to relax."

A warm hand on her shoulder replaced the cool water she'd thought surrounded her. She wanted his arms around her, but sharp needles in her arms prevented her from lifting her hands to touch Evan without pain.

Evan noticed and moved his hand from her shoulder to her hand. Her body relaxed even more, her thoughts slowing from the rapid cascade of her nightmare to a less panicked speed. Evan couldn't breathe underwater without scuba gear. He wore his uniform though, all black, even for nighttime operations.

She tried to look around, but the clamp prevented her from moving her head. When she asked, "where am I," it came out in a clump of gurgled sounds, not unlike water boiling.

Evan must have understood because he shushed her as the frantic activity in the room slowed.

"Don't talk. You're on a modified ventilator. You started breathing through your gills, but you can't do that here. The ventilator is keeping your gills closed, so you have to breathe through your nose."

His voice soothed her even further as she recognized the bareness of a hospital room. The waves of blue around her were the nurses handling her. None of that mattered though. With forced effort, she ordered her body to close her gills so she could breathe through her nose and talk as she would in the surface world.

"They dropped another grenade."

His hand tightened around hers. She couldn't even wince as his fingers squeezed the syndactyly between her fingers.

"I pushed as hard as I could, forcing it down, away from the damn Alts. I should have let it detonate under them. I should have focused on the dolphin pod. If I had..."

"If you had, what?" Evan asked, his voice as gentle as the tickle of sea grass against her body.

"If I had let the anti-Alts die, I could have saved my friend. The dolphin with the scarf. I always brought extra scarves with me so we could play together. He followed the grenade, thinking it was another game."

Evan said nothing. Just held her hand, his thumb rubbing

her knuckles as she cried again, easier now that she breathed through her nose. He said nothing more until she wound down. Once the tears stopped, he pulled her hand next to his cheek.

She hadn't noticed that the rest of the medical team caring for her had left the room, so she could be alone with Evan.

"What do we do now?" she asked, wiping away the tears from her face with the corner of the flimsy sheet covering her.

"What do you want to do now?"

Her anger flared. She wanted to find those anti-Alts and pound the bastards until their guts spilled out of their rotting carcasses. What she wanted, however, would never happen because the anti-Alts would be in police custody. They would go on trial in Thunder City. Their faces would be on the news for months and she would have to watch it all, maybe even testify.

Of course, she couldn't testify if they couldn't find her. Maybe she would follow through with her desire: swim out to the bay and never return. Leave the surface world behind, but that would mean leaving Evan behind, too.

He watched her, his hazel eyes soft, almost as if he knew what she was thinking. She never could hide her feelings from anyone. Submerged in Mystic Bay, she never had to.

What did she want? How could she explain her feeling to another person, to a man who couldn't live half of the life she craved? "I want to be alone, but I also want to share my life with someone. I don't want to be ignored, but I don't want people to stare at me. I want the freedom to live how I please, but I don't want to not be there for others if they need me. I want justice, but I'm too angry to be rational about it. And I want to change my moniker. I'm more than just my gills."

She had to stop to take a breath, her movement still limited by the ventilator. "I don't know what I want."

Was Evan upset? Sad? Disappointed that she couldn't give him a loving home and hearth, just like the one he'd been raised in? No, of course not. He was Evan Blackwood——playboy, billionaire, and hero to everyone in Thunder City. Most folks wouldn't even mistake him for his twin. They would just know by the way he talked, or the way he moved, or the way he looked at people when they wanted his attention, without getting distracted by odd features.

"It's okay to not know what you want. I don't know what I want. I had thought maybe we could both explore what we want together."

Explore together? It sounded so comforting. Wasn't that what every girl dreamed of? Wasn't that what she had dreamed of until she realized she would never be satisfied with just living in the surface world? She'd had dreams, before she'd crushed them so it wouldn't hurt so damn much when she realized they would never come true.

Maybe it was time to rekindle those dreams? Evan still held her hand. He didn't seem to mind, or even to realize what he was doing. He looked at her as if she were the only person in the room who mattered to him.

Hope flared, spreading through her heart, the flames burning away the resentment and hurt. She squeezed his hand back, forgetting about the ventilator wrapped around her gills, the throb of pain from the stitches in her forehead, the bloody marks elsewhere on her body from where the shrapnel hit her.

"I would love to explore the possibilities with you."

The crazy grin on his face reminded her of why he was such a heartthrob. This time, though, he was *her* heartthrob, and she wasn't going to let him go.

He leaned over the ventilator to kiss her, not with the overabundance of passion she would have liked. That would be too much for a flimsy hospital bed, with the IV still attached to her arm. Later, though, she would have her way with him.

"Let's see if we can get the doctors to release you from this..." He tapped the ventilator.

"We're lucky this hospital even has one."

Before Evan finished the sentence, the privacy curtain pulled back. Captain Spectacular stood there, looking even more intimidating than usual. "Evan, I need a word with you."

Evan kissed her fingertips. "I'll be right back."

She needed clothes after shedding her own in the bay, along with her apartment key and driver's license. Ugh. At least she could get the spare key she kept at T-CASS headquarters. The license would require more time, but it wasn't like she needed to drive a lot. Maybe Evan could fly her to the seaquarium and back every day? That thought held so many possibilities.

The pain of losing her dolphin friend still choked her. The anti-Alts would pay for what they did; she'd see to that. Visions of dropping the bastards into the middle of an oceanic whitetip frenzy appealed to her. That would teach them not to kill Alts, and one of her dolphins.

No, it wouldn't. The anti-Alts wouldn't care. They would see the dolphin as collateral damage in their war against the alternative humans. The end justified the means, and they had succeeded in killing at least twenty-five Alts in their attack on the harbor. They would celebrate their kills while sitting in jail awaiting trial. They would die in prison, heroes to their friends back in Star Haven.

Juan would care.

Where the hell did that thought come from?

He helped the Alts escape Star Haven. It's not his fault they died. He honestly looked upset about it.

Yeah, but he only saved them so he wouldn't have to live with them.

And you have to live with the Norms in Thunder City. The Norms who helped you this afternoon on cargo ship. The Norms who rescued you from the bay. Juan can't go back home to Star Haven. He has to live in Thunder City with you.

So, she was supposed to feel sorry for him? Screw that.

Screw you. Your own parents fled Star Haven without any help. He tried. He saved Hannah too. He can change. He can't do that if you don't help him. He can't do that if you never accept him.

I don't know if I can do that.

You don't know that you can't. Try it and maybe you won't be so damn angry all the time. You might actually make some friends outside of T-CASS. Your own friends, not just Evan's.

What if Juan doesn't want to change? What if he's... just like me, living here, but wanting to be elsewhere?

That's his problem, not yours.

The lump in her throat wouldn't help her convince the doctor to remove her ventilator. She had a lot of thinking to do. Juan was Cory Blackwood's partner. Cory was Evan's brother. If she wanted live in Evan's world, she had to get along with his friends and family. Everyone loved Evan, so there were probably lots of Norms in his life.

She needed to relax her body, put the emotion behind her where no one else could see it. Well, no one else but Evan. He would know what she felt, even if she had to tell him. She trusted him more than she loved him. Or, maybe that was part of loving someone who loved you back. Trust came with the package and she had just opened the biggest present she'd ever received, complete with sparkly wrapping paper and a huge red bow.

She could do this—for Evan, she could make peace with Norms—at least in Thunder City. Even the ones who stared at her. Possibly Juan too.

Her grief eased just as Evan returned. He didn't hesitate to pull the chair back to her bedside and take her hand back in his.

"Some good news. The doctor said now that you're

conscious, and you're all stitched up, they can release you to go home tonight."

She couldn't help the small smile. "I'll still need clothes. Mine are on the bottom of the bay, along with the key to my apartment."

"Just tell me your size. I'll get you clothes." He didn't hesitate with his answer.

"How? All the stores will be closed."

"I'll call Anthony Roberto. He'll open the store for me."

Gillian almost choked. "You mean Anthony Roberto of *Roberto and Vaughn?* At the mall?"

This time Evan kissed her forehead, careful to not touch the bandage over her stitches. "He knows my family. It's not the first time we've needed to get an emergency set clothes for folks."

Of course, Evan would be able to call the owner of the most upper-class clothing store in the city. The store she had only shopped at once, for a cousin's wedding. The dress had cost more than two months' rent and utilities put together. It had been the least expensive dress she could find there.

"It would be easier if you just talked to the manager of my apartment complex. He could let you inside. Maybe even give you a spare key."

"And give up an opportunity to spoil my girlfriend? Nope. You're getting a new wardrobe tonight. We'll leave the spare clothes at my apartment."

"Is that what you tell all of the other girls?"

He at least had the courtesy to wrinkle his nose. "Don't think about them. You're the girl for me, and once you move in, the world will know it."

"Oh, now I'm living with you. Just like that." Amazing how quickly she shifted from murderous rage and grief, to confusion, to wanting to dance through the hospital.

"Just like that." Evan repeated. "I also have more good news."

"I can't imagine what more good news you could have, beyond you getting all alpha male on me, and informing me that I'm moving into your apartment."

He had the grace to at least blush. "Yeah, well, some girls like it when I'm a Neanderthal."

"It is adorable; just don't make it a habit."

"Deal." He pulled back a little and readjusted himself on the hospital chair, which even from the corner of her eye looked uncomfortable. "I got a call from one of the EMTs who brought you in here. He heard you talk about the dolphin who got hurt from the explosion. He mentioned it online, without giving a lot of details. He got a response from a rescue group who'd received a call from couple who were enjoying a romantic evening on the beach far south of the warehouse. A dolphin had beached itself there and it was bleeding. The rescue group was able to transport the dolphin to the seaquarium. He's hurt, but alive. They're going to keep him until he heals."

"Oh, Evan!" The tears started again as her heart beat faster to near bursting. "That's wonderful news. I'll go there tomorrow. He'll be scared. I can calm him down. I'll bring more scarves. Could you get me more scarves at *Roberto & Vaughn*?"

If he was horrified at paying those prices for scarves that would be sitting in a tank with a dolphin, he didn't show it.

"I'll get you get you so many colorful scarves, you'll be buried from your toes to your nose in them." His playful tone turned serious again. "Mom has also called for a meeting tomorrow at the estate. Family only. If you feel up to it, I want you to be there."

She almost stopped breathing again. Damn, she needed to get this ventilator off her neck. "I'm not family."

"I consider you family. You will be family soon, so it's just a technicality at this point."

It took her a second to figure out what he was saying. "That has got to be the most unromantic proposal ever."

"I'll make it up to you. I promise. Will you go with me? To the meeting."

"Evan Blackwood, I will follow you anywhere."

"Gillian Sands, you won't have to follow me. You will be by my side forever."

He kissed her then, keeping it soft and gentle and perfect. Without having to say "yes," she knew would be staying by his side forever, even if it meant living in the surface world. They would both heal and live the rest of their lives together.

COMING in 2026!
BLOOD AVENGER
The final book in the Thunder City saga. All of your favorite characters join together for the final epic battle against the Court of Blood.

In the meantime, check out the first chapter of DREAM OF MY SOUL

A vampire must protect the world's only vampire hunter (who happens to be her ex-fiancé) from the demon who hunts both of them.

***

***

The chilled wind whisked between the headstones as it plucked the dead oak leaves from the ground. Under the winter's moon the gust picked up speed and began to circle and spin until the small dust devil settled on a corner of the graveyard, a space not marked by granite or covered in ice. Through the thick, red Georgia clay a portal punched through to this world disrupting the whirlwind. It started small, barely a pinprick, but the power that leaked through from the other side scattered a family of raccoons and silenced the crickets as all the creatures that called this cemetery home stilled.

From the other side the demon whispered.

***

VINCENZIA DUG her fingernails into the soft leather of the van's steering wheel as a soft voice caressed her skin. She checked the rear view mirror, but nothing had changed. In the back seat, Bryce pounded away at his laptop trying to figure out if the old Victorian home they surveilled had a network he could hack. Ilario, in the passenger seat, studied the Victorian's blueprints, his elven eyes as sensitive in the dark as her own. On his shoulder, Rosemary flicked one of her dragonfly wings in boredom.

"What's wrong?" Ilario asked, as he set aside his tablet.

Of course he noticed her shiver, but Vincenzia didn't answer. Instead she glanced at the Victorian. Even from four blocks away she could tell no one was home. Lamplight lit one south facing room, but even her preternatural eyesight couldn't see through the heavy curtains. The sea breeze blew steady off the Atlantic and threaded through the palms of the ordinary, upper-class St. Augustine neighborhood.

The voice hadn't come from their target.

"It's nothing," she replied. "I thought Bryce had said something."

Bryce grunted in response as his fingers increased their speed. In the reflection of the driver's side window, Ilario's unsatisfied concern stared back at her. If Bryce, as large in human form as he was as a wolf, had spoken, half the neighborhood would have heard him.

The voice was probably a wayward ghost. In St. Augustine, Florida, you couldn't hit a stoplight without running through one spirit or another. Even though none of the apparitions she'd encountered over the centuries had ever spoken to her it wasn't impossible for her to hear the dead.

After all, she was a vampire and dead as they came.

Ilario, a sea elf with blue-silver hair, was her self-appointed guardian and far more sensitive to such beings than a vampire, even one still in possession of a soul shard. Yet, he didn't appear to have heard the voice at all.

"I got nothing." Bryce slammed the laptop closed, his chevron mustache framing his frown. "If the Believers live there, they must not have set up shop yet. There's nothing for me to hack, not even cable TV."

"Maybe it's not them?" Rosemary stood up and stretched, releasing her dark hair so it cascaded along her shoulders. Ilario reached up and stroked a finger down the pixie's back in sympathy, triggering a release of her sparkling dust onto his shoulder.

Was it possible that the clandestine group of elf watchers had decided not to set up a cell here in the Ancient City? Ilario was certain he saw one of the Elders while he fueled their roundabout at the marina. Another shiver let loose more worry that she tried to hide. Even if Bryce couldn't confirm their location tonight, none of them could risk exposure.

Forty years after their rogue family put down roots in Florida, it was time to leave. She would lose another home, watch it plunge into the ocean as Ilario sunk their little island he'd built to keep her safe. No matter how many times they'd fled and rebuilt, it never got easier.

Damn the Believers. Nothing would make Vincenzia happier than to kick their asses all the way back to Venice and maybe spill some of their blood along the way. As if he'd read her mind, Ilario reached over and as gently as he had with Rosemary, ran a finger along her cheek. Comforted from his touch, Vincenzia closed her eyes. Deep inside her soul shard pulsed, repressing her violent nature, keeping it locked tight.

"Let's head home," he said.

Despite her desire to lean into the warmth of Ilario's touch, she turned the key in the ignition. Before she could release the brake, the voice returned again, louder, more forceful this time, drowning out the noise from the engine.

The word it whispered was distinct: *Vincenzia.*

ALSO BY DEBRA JESS

If you like Science Fiction, check out the complete Heroes of Andromeda series starting with ANDROMEDA'S REBEL:

They took the sky from her, and her memory, but no one could take away her rebellious spirit.

If you prefer Urban Fantasy, DREAM OF MY SOUL is now available.

A vampire must protect the world's only vampire hunter (who also happens to be her ex-fiancé) from the demon who hunts both of them.

ACKNOWLEDGMENTS

When A Secret Love debuted last year, the idea of finishing and publishing A Secret Life seemed so far out of reach, it tired me just to think about it. I persisted despite my own doubts and as you can see, A Secret Life now has a life of its own.

I couldn't have gotten here without the support of two amazing editors, Debra Doyle who has been with me since the beginning, and Erica Monroe who has worked on the last two books. Thank you both for helping me through my Thunder City journey.

ABOUT THE AUTHOR

A Connecticut Yankee transplanted to Central Florida, Debra Jess writes science fiction romance, science fantasy, superheroes, and urban fantasy. She began writing in 2006, combining her love of fairy tales and Star Wars to craft original stories of ordinary people in extraordinary adventures and fantastical creatures in out-of-this world escapades. Along the way she's acquired a love for stray cats, flower gardens, and traveling for her own adventures. You can follow Debra Jess's adventures by subscribing to her newsletter on her website

Facebook
Instagram
Threads
Bluesky